ASCENT TO OMAI

ALSO BY WILSON HARRIS

Fiction:
Palace of the Peacock
Far Journey of Oudin
The Whole Armour
The Secret Ladder
Heartland
The Eye of the Scarecrow
The Waiting Room
Tumatumari
The Age of the Rainmakers
Black Marsden
Companions of the Day and Night
Da Silva da Silva's Cultivated Wilderness and Genesis of the Clowns
The Tree of the Sun
The Angel at the Gate
Carnival
The Infinite Rehearsal
The Four Banks of the River of Space
Resurrection at Sorrow Hill
Jonestown
The Dark Jester
The Mask of the Beggar
The Ghost of Memory

Poetry:
Fetish
Eternity to Season

ASCENT TO OMAI

WILSON HARRIS

INTRODUCTION BY MICHAEL MITCHELL

PEEPAL TREE

First published by Faber & Faber
in Great Britain in 1970
Republished in 2018 by
Peepal Tree Press Ltd
17 King's Avenue
Leeds LS6 1QS
England

ISBN13: 9781845233549

Supported by
ARTS COUNCIL
ENGLAND

For
Margaret, my wife and
Charles Monteith

Life is never religious but it becomes religious as subsistence of memory and crucifixion of appetite.

– Anonymous

Since "adventure" and "science" have led over many centuries to the denigration of humanity, robot law, unfeeling yoke, there is no ground of alternatives but to recover the "dangerous" chasm, the "forbidden" ascent and seek a new dimension of *feeling* – a new oath of humanity.

– Victor's Bible

CONTENTS

INTRODUCTION

MICHAEL MITCHELL

In Memoriam Wilson Harris 1921-2018

To say that *Ascent to Omai* is a quest by a son to find his lost father, during the course of which he finds himself, might make it sound like a banal Hollywood animation. But, in a novel by Wilson Harris, there is always more, and seeing how *much* more there is, is the nature of the arts. "Art is seeing things," says a character in Ali Smith's novel *Winter*. "Where would we be without our ability to see beyond what it is we're supposed to be seeing."[1]

A son's quest for a father, and a process of self-discovery, are all about identity and time. Traditional novels trace the development of identifiable characters through time, assuming that the borders of character are fixed and the relationships between characters are definable at any time. They also assume a fixed scale of passing time – which may involve flashbacks and foreshadowing – but which provides a stable frame to which the plot can be attached. But what if our understanding of time and space is held prisoner by a consciousness that is bounded by our inability to perceive beyond the three dimensions of the material world and what we experience as the passing of time? What if the stability of the material world, revealed at the atomic and sub-atomic levels to be subject to unexpected symbioses and feedback mechanisms, is also affected by how human beings perceive it? What if time is relative within an expanding but finite curvature of space? To describe such a world, a different type of novel is needed.

Wilson Harris realized this, and Hena Maes-Jelinek, in one of a pair of highly perceptive studies of the novel, writes that *Ascent to Omai*, first published in 1970, represents "his most daring experiment so far with the form of the novel".[2] Harris uses various techniques to destabilize our ideas of time and identity. If we take character to begin with, *Ascent to Omai* opens with one character pursuing another up a hillside towards a ridge, or watershed. One, the focus of consciousness, is named Victor. The other, who at times appears to be an illusion composed of weather and landscape, is described as Victim. Later Victor realizes that he is pursuing his own ghost, or his father. His father, Adam – unaccommodated man – is a struggling factory worker, a welder who goes on strike, burns down the factory and his own home before being tried and imprisoned. On his release, he goes to seek his fortune in the Guyanese interior. Victor himself is congruent with the judge at the trial, who is to die in an aircraft crash. At the trial the prosecution and defence lawyers are representatives of different modes of perception, and a number of characters, or aliases, give evidence, some of them springing from the judge's own imagination in the form of sketches on cards, which he shuffles in a pack. The apparently arbitrary nature of character makes sense if we see that true empathy involves participation in all aspects of ourselves, both positive and negative, and thus a constant process of self-confession and self-judgement. In this sense Victor is also Adam, but with the potential to move beyond him through a growth in consciousness, which is the matter of the novel.

A second dimension in this process is in understanding the actual stages in the relationship between father and son, which are inseparable from the stages of growing consciousness. In *Ascent to Omai* these stages are symbolized in the image of ripples in water spreading out from a central event (see p. 97, this edition). Each event horizon corresponds with the death of the previous stage of personality. In this diagrammatic representation the centre (the stone) represents both birth – a traumatic event for both Adam and Victor because the mother died in childbirth – and the birth of consciousness prompted by the stone which cuts the falling toddler and constitutes his first memory. The petticoat, standing vicariously for the absent mother, is where the child hid from his drunken father, and where he was given a blow while he watched his father having sex with a prostitute. The whale represents the phase in which the boy used to wait for his father outside the factory. Rose is associated with the sailor who moves beyond the boy's initially limited horizons. Iron mask represents anonymity hiding royal potential. The three animal transformations (Parrot, Raven and Baboon) then lead out to Madonna, or Muse, reconnecting with the absent feminine. It is striking that this diagram corresponds with Renaissance alchemical imagery, and it is described as the "factory of the gilded man", created gradually from the *prima materia*. The goal of the alchemists was also described as the *lapis*, the (philosopher's) stone. So the stone at the centre of the diagram is both beginning and end, as the ripples from a stone dropped in water are the record and constant presence of the originary event.

This alternative view of time, the second destabilizing factor in comparison with the traditional novel, corresponds with what we know of pre-Columbian conceptions, in which time was visualized as concentric circles or spirals, or as parallel lines, each allowing access to both past and future from the present.[3] It is for this reason that time, not as an abstract concept of measurement, but as a spectre which can be either a vessel of humanity or its gaol, becomes central to the design of the novel. (cf. p. 88). The judge, speaking vicariously for the author, tells the reader: "He wanted, he knew, to write a kind of novel or novel history in which the spectre of time was the main character, and the art of narrative the obsessed ground/lighthouse of security/insecurity." (p. 90) Here the boundaries between character, narrator and author are also breached, so that the destablization of identity extends out as far as the author, and, to the extent that the reader is forced through the style of writing to participate in the construction of meaning, to the reader as well.

However, the author does not appear as a didactic presence. Instead, he lays out the novel in a series of theatrical or cinematic scenes threaded by a resonating texture of metaphor. It may help the reader to summarize these, as they shape the course of the novel as it proceeds, but do not correspond exactly with the chapter or section divisions.

The first is the ascent towards the watershed, in which Victor pursues the spectral shape of his father. We should note here how not only time, character and narration are destabilized but also space, for although the reader can visualize the scene perfectly, Book I bears the title "Omai Chasm"; so is it above or below? While climbing he is hit by something, which causes him to fall and change his perception. At this point Victor's memories begin.

His first memories are of his childhood in the poor Georgetown district of Albuoystown and of hiding in the petticoat. There follow memories of school, and shining light from the setting sun via a mirror into his father's eyes when he came out of the factory. This leads to memories of the strike and the arson attack.

While Victor continues to climb the hill, and recalls the trial itself, he reaches the claim established by Adam to prospect for minerals. The claim is marked by an overgrown piece of tin from a wrecked aircraft. At this point the trial is remembered by Victor as judge, travelling in the aircraft which will be wrecked on Omai. The trial is described in some detail, with submissions from counsel for the prosecution and the defence, and witnesses including a psychiatrist, Dr Wall. As evidence a poem called "Fetish"[4] is presented. The memories of the trial are associated with cards the judge is shuffling as he sits on the aircraft.

The narration now returns to the child's development and the image of the ripples from the stone, as it shifts into epistolatory form and theatrical dialogue, which close Book II. Book III, in the form of a coda, recapitulates the images of the ripples, now as a metanarration referring back to the page numbers in the novel,[5] before the judge shuffles his cards again to suggest an infinity of alternative possibilities. The novel closes as he moves towards his own death and the final vision of the father fighting the blaze which he started, with the remnants of the mother's petticoat clinging to him and disintegrating, but offering a faint hope of redemption.

★ ★ ★

Because Wilson Harris is working with a new type of novel form, which may be unfamiliar to some readers, it is perhaps useful to suggest two aids to reading. Both involve the image. Hena Maes-Jelinek suggested that what Harris was doing could be compared to "an abstract painting whose components would have the capacity to move".[6] Understanding the way he uses both linguistic imagery – metaphor, association, ambiguity, punning, allusive resonances – as well as intertextuality is a key to reading his work and seeing how it is possible to overcome the contraints of the conventional novel form. Let's take an example from the beginning of the book and see how that works in practice. This passage opens with Victor pursuing another, as yet nameless, man up towards the watershed. A watershed is a point of suspended alternatives, where water-drops may take opposite paths to the sea. The image thus represents how apparent diversity may have origins and ends in identity. This idea is repeated later in the novel as the origin of the ripples from a singular event caused by a stone:

> Ascending the hill above the river towards a spectral watershed compounded of vague mists, vague solid: part moisture, vague sky. *Patron saint of the watershed*. A beam of sun like stained glass window pierced the rain-sodden atmosphere: the diffuse character of the environment seemed to embody the figure of the scarecrow, ruined porknocker, ascending the hill. Rags of gold. He stopped and looked back over his shoulder at Victor who trailed behind. A black memorable wreath of a face. White-bearded. Memorable because it seemed almost faceless. Like a slate. Upon which a beard of chalk had been drawn and within which holes for eyes had been punched with cracks around them, wrinkles and cracks. Through the holes the misty wreath of mingled

jungle and sky shone. A faceless face whose soul of slate was instinct with the warp of a universal element. Peculiar *tabula rasa*. VICTIM. Victor half-laughed, half-cursed. He felt he had partially drawn the victim there himself upon the slate of nature, partially drawn it with fire and partially erased it, partially sponged it with water.

The ruined figure resumed its flight on the hill like someone falling up a ladder, looking back all the while. It seemed to Victor that the slate of his head cracked still farther around his eyes leaving a blank space all of a sudden where his features had been; and this implosive character- istic began in turn to eat downwards into his shoulders and to his middle like a gigantic collapsing globule, portrait of rain and chalk.

There remained only his stalwart legs like trees walking up the hill, ragged trousers of leaves. But blue rather than green, blue leaves within a forest of cloud. Blue like the discarded tattered uniform of a police constable. All at once he dislodged a couple of stones like a sentryman's boots and these raced downhill so swiftly they struck Victor a heavy blow on the brow before he could avert it. *Constable of the watershed.* It was a grim ironic clout and kick on the heels of an earlier assumption – patron saint of the watershed… When Victor regained consciousness after the blow he had been dealt – like one arising from a dream – the ruined constable had vanished. Was it a mirage of the senses, *doppelgänger,* self-appointed ruin compounded of his own losses and gains? He too (Victor) had made a fortune in the gold and diamond fields of the interior but had lost every- thing in the end …. (pp. 25-26)

Here Harris creates an immensely vivid representation of an ascent on a mountainside in the Guyanese interior, but uses imagery to allude to opposites, analogies, correspondences and contrasts which only subsequent reading will unlock. There is the victor/victim contrast, relativized by the word "wreath", normally used for the victor, placed on the victim's brows, but also connected to death and funerals. The sun, cloud and vegetation all evoke allusive elements of religious apotheosis, secular control (constable), a nebulous cloudy face as a mask but also chalk-slate available to palimpsest re-writing. Evocations of earth, air, fire and water as well as gold direct the reader towards porknocker prospectors, mythical Eldorado and alchemical transformation. Three foreign language terms point up distinctive elements: the first two are the *tabula rasa* of revolutionary representation (daring experiment) and the *doppelgänger* which will be expanded to show that the figure Victor is pursuing is his father Adam, the representative of suffering humanity in the material world, but that they are aspects of a single being, judge and convict, oppressor and oppressed. The ascent is also a descent ("like someone falling up a ladder"), and the Omai of the novel's title is simultaneously a summit and a chasm, an Amerindian name, a transitory "mushroom" settlement and a colloquial exclamation. The third term, appearing a little later, is *opus contra naturam*, a work against nature, recalling the need both to upset the natural order laid down by convention and also the name given by alchemists to the alchemical process itself.

The combination of cloud and trousers will be taken up as an allusion to Mayakovsky's Modernist poem "A Cloud in Trousers", particularly in connection with the Russian Revolution,[7] and we find out later that Adam worked as a welder before being involved in the strike and setting fire to the factory as well as his own "bed and board". As a widower he had consoled himself with a "woman from the streets", giving his young son, who was hiding for safety in his dead mother's petticoat, a drunken "clout" in the side for disturbing them by crying. This is prefigured in our passage by the stone dislodged from Adam's boot, which becomes a fruitful trauma and provokes a procession of actions represented later by the expanding ripples. From a mirror (or wound, an allusion to Christ's wound) in his side the adolescent boy takes to shining a beam of light in his father's eyes, an image for what is happening in the novel as a whole. As he climbs, Victor sees the sun glinting on an aircraft. This could be the one in which the judge, recollecting the conviction of Adam, is travelling towards a crash. It is from the wreckage of this plane that the metal sign Victor finds marking Adam's abandoned claim has been constructed. Mayakovsky's poem is specifically linked with the name of Donne ("Encircling vestments of poetry – Donne to Mayakovsky", p. 27), shared by the enigmatic central figure of Harris's first published novel *Palace of the Peacock*, but here used to stress a continuity between three poets: the revolutionary Renaissance poet from the brief flowering of Gnostic sensibility before the onset of orthodoxies of Puritan fundamentalism and scientific materialism, the revolutionary poet of futurist Modernism, and in addition the poem apparently written by Adam/Victor but actually by Harris, which so puzzles the participants at Adam's trial.

This should be enough to illustrate how Harris uses the moving play of imagery to decentre his novel and allow fascinating combinations to compose themselves during reading, although it requires reading both backwards and forwards as well as the use of the imagination, not simply as the locus for the formation of images, but more importantly as a faculty of openness to mystery through which the author motivates the reader to revise chains of causality in personal lives, in philosophical and psychological abstractions, in the history of societies and even the geological and evolutionary history of the planet itself.

★ ★ ★

Another approach to the novel is by way of the visual image. The judge refers to the sketches he made during the trial (using charcoal, a drawing material that has been through fire), relating them to what Cézanne called "*ma petite sensation*". Cézanne used this phrase to describe how he learnt to comprehend a reality beyond surfaces, beyond what it was he was supposed to be seeing, and to use paint on canvas to convey this to the viewer. In 2014 the distinguished Guyanese artist Stanley Greaves completed a sequence of 24 paintings entitled "Dialogue with Wilson Harris", one of which, "Georgetown to Omai" gives us a unique opportunity to study a cross-disciplinary response to Harris's work.[8]

Georgetown to Omai
Stanley Greaves

In the painting we see two tiny stylized figures on the right, whose indeterminacy has multiplied them into a third within a sort of burning bush, climbing up towards a sky with a tiny aeroplane in it. At the bottom of the picture the welder on the left holds a torch which is starting a fire, but the torch seems like a garter on the thigh of a woman dressed in the green of vegetation. The open legs of the woman suggest a chasm, whose red and black hues reflect both the welder's muscular body and vertical of the spine and also the fault-line which divides the whole picture. The body of the woman leads up to two representations of heads, one with a black halo of hair and the indications of two eyes, the other a black sun filled with chalky cloud placed above a broken and bleeding neckline. This forms a part of a series of offset arcs echoing the colours used throughout the painting, within which the boy seems to be hiding, almost touched by a disembodied protective arm. These arcs form the voluminous maternal petticoat, but they also suggest the ripples caused by the falling stone, which would find their centre in the womb of the woman's body, and the strata of rock in the landscape.

Extending through the welder's head and mask and what seems to be a sapphire blue mirror is the spear of light shining up to a second mirror held in the boy's hand, while the boy's eyes appear to gaze up and beyond to where the aircraft approaches the summit. Framed within the body of the boy, to the left of the saw-toothed fault-line, and thus directly in the line of the spear, there are the luminous silhouettes in black of the participants in the trial scene, while, above the boy, chalky clouds are like ripples in dark water. Contrasting with the curves and arcs above the woman (who with the dual head combines the role of whore and Madonna – in the novel the outermost ripple from the stone), the upward-striving welder is backed by straight, masculine metal lines, emphasizing a contrast between manufacture and nature. His torch, like a phallic symbol, attacks his own bed and board. If we follow the rays of the sky back they lead to the central trial scene, suggesting the origin of Victor's judgmental attitude towards his father, which is to be revised during the ascent. Ascent is stressed in the movement from lower left to upper right, but the movement of the legs, echoed by the tiny figures, indicates a centre of gravity within the woman which tends to fall back towards the bottom left, so that descent (to Omai chasm) is contained within Ascent (to Omai). The slight tilt of the vertical fault-line is balanced by the heads and the black orb, which could represent the eye of the void.

The void is a recurring trope in Harris's work[9]. A void is often taken to have merely negative connotations (*contra naturam*), an aporia resulting from the postmodern absence of grand narratives. Yet Donne's contemporary Shakespeare was fascinated by the void, by the relationship between everything and nothing, being and non-being. King Lear infamously announces at the beginning of the play that "nothing will come of nothing", but is then forced to discover that everything comes of it, and that what he regarded as everything in terms of worldly power, social and human relationships or bodily faculties is nothing, as he is gradually reduced to a "bare, forked animal", and yet the whimper that ends his howling despair is infinitely more moving and substantial than Nahum Tate's happy ending.[10] Shakespeare knew that the "wooden O", the zero or void, when combined with the crooked figure of the imagination, could produce the whole world, the Globe. Harris's novels frequently contain theatres, and the process within them is an "infinite rehearsal". The void, a place without space or time, allows access to other lives and ages in a way that the frame of the Newtonian universe does not permit, whereas in the universe of quantum physics, the quantum particle can be simultaneously present and on the other side of the universe. Thus, for Harris, the void is a space pregnant with possible conceptions.

★ ★ ★

Of course, in exploring spaces of the imagination, a writer may be accused of neglecting political realities. Indeed, comparisons between Wilson Harris and Martin Carter have centred on a contrast between "Carter's avowed resistance and Harris's dissatisfaction with protest".[11] Yet in many ways *Ascent to Omai* is an overtly political novel. Victor, risen to a high position in society, where he can be comfortably ensconsed in an aircraft above his father's derelict claim, has the luxury of daydreaming through much of Adam's trial; Adam, with his background of poverty and exploitation, can easily been seen as a representative of proletarian victims of both colonialism and capitalism, and indeed set against them as a protagonist of wider revolutionary action: "Victor felt as he studied the legend of his father, fresh from slavery, fresh from the factory, rum-soaked labour (Boxing Day overtime) that here was the masked creator of Insurrection Day long before the Russian Revolution, Lenin or Trotsky, Stalin or Devil." (p. 39) But Adam's action in burning down the factory and then his own home are portrayed as self-destructive. As Sailor points out: "We're slaves to industry. Slaves to factory. Slaves to monotony. Slaves to desk. Slaves to fortune. It's ironic but because we believe in the heights of the banal and overlook the depths of royalty (dispossessed claim) we lose a vocation for freedom, for originality" (p. 118). Seen in this way, only chance determines who has a fortune and who is a slave, and revolution, under such an unimaginative stasis of thought, will merely reverse the roles. This echoes Harris's critique of C.L.R. James in his essay *History, Fable and Myth in the Caribbean and the Guianas* (1970). James claimed that J.J. Thomas's *Froudacity* (1889) had "overwhelmed" Froude's racist thesis in *The English in the West Indies, or The Bow of Ulysses* (1888). Harris indeed takes apart Froude's conservative view of history as a "philosophy of fortuitous achievement, dicey establishment, realm of accident", but then argues that Thomas remains within the same philosophy of chance (whether particular governors or magistrates were favourable or unfavourable to the advance of Caribbean Blacks), and this failing he instances as an example of the "historical stasis which has afflicted the Caribbean I would suggest for many generations" (p. 6).[12] This is why the author chooses to make Victor and Adam different aspects of the same person. Without a spiritual development, a vocation for freedom and originality, political action will not succeed. When Harris includes Adam's poem "Fetish", one of Harris's own poems from his first published collection in 1951, he alludes to something expressed in a letter to A J Seymour: "In Fetish I was concerned with the fact that the structures of civilisation man has built have become oppressive, since it has not been built in true accord with the energies or creative forms at its roots. Those sources therefore are bound to establish a distorted connection — sardonic, violent, protesting…" Gemma Robinson concludes: "Harris promotes alternative worlds in which imagination acts not to palliate people's suffering in the material world, but to cure that world".[13]

The journey Harris sends the reader on is a perilous quest. As he says in the second epigraph: "there is no ground of alternatives but to recover the 'dangerous' chasm, the 'forbidden' ascent and seek a new dimension of *feeling* – a new oath of humanity". The judge says he is seeking a "qualitative illumination" rather than "heights of the banal" (p. 118). It is a quest for the " *one* frail thread – call it unity, call it love – within and beyond all" (p. 87). Derek Attridge[14] points out that a work of literature should be seen not as an object but as an event in which the reader participates, through which the serious writer strives to bring about changes in the culture by changing the reader. It is in such an adventurous spirit that *Ascent to Omai* should be read.

Endnotes

1.   Ali Smith, *Winter* (London: Hamish Hamilton, 2017), pp. 216 ff.
2.   Hena Maes-Jelinek, *The Labyrinth of Universality* (Amsterdam and New York: Rodopi, 2006), p. 205.
3.   See, for example, Francisco Seoane and María José Culquichicón-Venegas, 'Hitching the Present to the Stars: The Architecture of Time and Space in the Ancient Andes', in Swensen and Roddick (eds.), *Constructions of Time and History in the Pre-Columbian Andes* (Louisville: University Press of Colorado, 2018): "Andean people thus appear to have understood the flow of time not

in terms of discontinuities, disruptions or breaks but in terms of the constant negotiations of intimate reciprocal exchanges."

4. Fetish is the title of Wilson Harris's first poetry collection, a chapbook, published under the pseudonym of Kona Waruk in 1951.

5. The page numbers in Harris's text to have been altered in this edition to be consistent with the content referred to.

6. Hena Maes-Jelinek, ibid., p. 205.

7. J.J. Healey, in 'Wilson Harris at Work: The Texas Manuscripts with Special Reference to the Mayakovsky Resonance in *Ascent to Omai*' in *Ariel* 15:4 (1984), 89-107, concludes that Mayakovsky's poem played a more prominent role in early drafts of the novel. There remain significant verbal connections, for instance, between "A Cloud in Trousers" and this novel, as in: "Suddenly,/ clouds/and various cloud-like things in the sky/will kick up a fuss,/as if white-suited workers were dispersing/after calling an embittered strike against the sky..." (*Russian Poetry: The Modern Period*, University of Iowa Press, 1978).

8. This is the painting used on the cover of this edition. See *Dialogue with Wilson Harris by Stanley Greaves* (Georgetown, Castellani House, 2014).

9. For example, in *Ascent to Omai*, after the references to Mayakovsky and Donne, Victor examines his conscience after the 'clout' as a "bump on his temples where he had been kicked a moment ago. *There was conscience. Dialectic of the boot.* A scar on his neck where he had been beheaded ages ago. *There was conscience. Metaphysics of the axe.* A kind of bodiless and yet bodily mystery he carried within – psyche of history. Stigmata of the void." (p. 27, original emphases).

10. In Nahum Tate's *King Lear* (1681), there is no Fool and the play ends with Cordelia and Edgar's marriage.

11. Gemma Robinson, "Vocabularies of Protest and Resistance: The Early Work of Wilson Harris and Martin Carter" in *Journal of Caribbean Literatures* 2, 1-3 (2000), 36-46, 36.

12. *History, Fable and Myth in the Caribbean and the Guianas* (Georgetown: National History and Arts Council, 1970, pp. 5-8.

12. Quoted in Robinson, ibid., 42.

13. Derek Attridge, *The Work of Literature* (Oxford: OUP, 2015).

BOOK I

OMAI CHASM

Noon saturated by rain when Victor saw the ruined porknocker, destitute miner, broken millionaire…

Ascending the hill above the river towards a spectral watershed compounded of vague mists, vague solid: part moisture, vague sky. *Patron saint of the watershed.* A beam of sun like stained glass window pierced the rain-sodden atmosphere: the diffuse character of the environment seemed to embody the figure of the scarecrow, ruined porknocker, ascending the hill. Rags of gold. He stopped and looked back over his shoulder at Victor who trailed behind. A black memorable wreath of a face. White-bearded. Memorable because it seemed almost faceless. Like a slate. Upon which a beard of chalk had been drawn and within which holes for eyes had been punched with cracks around them, wrinkles and cracks. Through the holes the misty wreath of mingled jungle and sky shone. A faceless face whose soul of slate was instinct with the warp of a universal element. Peculiar *tabula rasa*. VICTIM. Victor half-laughed, half-cursed. He felt he had partially drawn the victim there himself upon the slate of nature, partially drawn it with fire and partially erased it, partially sponged it with water.

The ruined figure resumed its flight on the hill like someone falling up a ladder, looking back all the while. It seemed to Victor that the slate of his head cracked still farther around his eyes leaving a blank space all of a sudden where his features had been; and this implosive characteristic began in turn to eat downwards into his shoulders and to his middle like a gigantic collapsing globule, portrait of rain and chalk.

There remained only his stalwart legs like trees walking up the hill, ragged trousers of leaves. But blue rather than green, blue leaves within a forest of cloud. Blue like the discarded tattered uniform of a police constable. All at once he dislodged a couple of stones like a sentryman's boots and these raced downhill so swiftly they struck Victor a heavy blow on the brow before he could avert it. *Constable of the watershed.* It was a grim ironic clout and kick on the heels of an earlier assumption – patron saint of the watershed… When Victor regained consciousness after the blow he had been dealt – like one arising from a dream – the ruined constable had vanished. Was it a mirage of the senses, *doppelgänger,* self-appointed ruin compounded of his own losses and gains ? He too (Victor) had made a fortune in the gold and diamond fields of the interior but had lost everything in the end…

He gave a shout – "You – you – up there. Where are you?"

No reply save an echo. Reverberation. Far beneath and far above. Axe to wood, walking tree. An echo which – menacing as it was in its spiral of height and depth – seemed to disperse a violent collision within man and nature, voice and element; seemed to muffle and arrest the blade of an organ, boot of a forehead, kick of an executioner, stone of insensibility. Victor groaned… awoke… struggled up and began again his slow dreaming ascent in pursuit of the vanished constable, saint and executioner of the watershed.

Beneath him lay the chasm of the river, volcanic and subdued. Above him stood the mountains of lava, worshipful and brooding, a subsidiary ridge of temperament thrusting – as he felt – towards loops of sky and bush. Topography of the heartland. Within one such loop – half-slate half-chalk of cloud – the sun appeared to vegetate, hanging in the sky. Suddenly straddled by its own vine and trousers, reformation of the loop – Victor felt himself addressed by a line from a

Russian poet – art of revolution – a *cloud in trousers*... Encircling vestments of poetry – Donne to Mayakovsky. Victor stopped to examine his own conscience in this respect – half-metaphysical, half-dialectical. A bump on his temples where he had been kicked a moment ago. *There was conscience. Dialectic of the boot.* A scar on his neck where he had been beheaded ages ago. *There was conscience. Metaphysics of the axe.* A kind of bodiless and yet bodily mystery he carried within – psyche of history. Stigmata of the void.

It was a question – he contorted his features in a clown's grimace – no one could shrug off, however misty, however intangible. The apprehension of age and conscience. The art of apportioning one's parts within a global wound, irreality. The sliding scale of death. Dead today and alive tomorrow. Condemned today. Reprieved tomorrow. The marriage of grotesque relations, doctor and patient, judge and judged, life and death, past and present... Victor resumed his funeral march towards the watershed. Noon to sunset. Within six hours he felt he would straddle the Amazon in pursuit of the reformation of the loop, a cloud in trousers.

It was a question of agencies. Agents – all of whom, however misguided, however perverse – were instruments beyond themselves, subconscious, involuntary perhaps, invoking a light of compassion within the abyss of history. Reformation of the loop. "Nonsense," Victor grumbled. "How can one begin to translate a fiend of a conqueror, an infernal conception into a mine of proportions – agency of compassion? Compassion of all things! It's absurd."

"*Subverted by compassion.*" It was the sigh of the wind on the hillside. A garish breath, the colour of transubstantiation, blood, shone through the clouds.

"Subverted my backside," Victor snapped with brutish vulgarity.

His secret companion sighed again and insisted – "One must view the conqueror," he said, "from the rear. Don't you see how innocent he is – a backhanded agent who exposes himself and appears to confirm (even as he denies) his own grotesque function. A kind of megalomaniac: child and sleep-walker who dreams of subjective filth. Dreams of an obscure order in which he was involved from the inception of con-quest, the inception of contamination, the inception of gold. An underground charter of consciousness. The higher one's achievement of glory and insulation, the deeper the abyss – prenatal abyss, postmortem abyss, post-dynastic abyss – which gnaws at one's liver. Liver of compassion."

"A grain of truth, who knows, in what you say," said Victor addressing his trousers which he had draped over a rock. He had stopped now on the hillside to defecate. "There may be something in it – that the landscape of history is constructed by a daemon of the heartland, daemon of internality, daemon of possession within nevertheless an ironic dislocating factor, half-forgotten instinct – *the constitution of humility*…"

Victor was not ashamed, facing his trousers on the hill, to talk to himself. It was something that happened to him quite frequently. Like writing a letter addressed to the public at large but meant for a secret agent, a secret companion within. The absurdity of the exercise bordered upon a religious conviction. A religious humour as well. A curious rehearsal with the elements. As if one day he would meet the ruined porknocker face to face, *doppelgänger* of the heartland, and since their conversation would entail speculations about the death as well as life of history, immortal as well as mortal values – he must prepare himself by every means at his disposal for such a dialogue.

Porknockers, in fact, Victor knew, had the most curious names. Insane really. Caesar, Kaiser, Bible, Encyclopaedia, etc. Capable too of dressing up in any sort of outlandish costume they could beg or borrow or scrape from the bottom of the barrel, fortune's barrel, odds and ends, rags and taxes. Sometimes they would appear quite naked in a mushroom village in the bush except for a constable's uniform they might whip from their haversack to make an impression or a District Commissioner's discarded helmet they might set at an angle upon their skulls – sometimes a cassock (of all things) like a renegade monk's pyjamas… Victor arose. Pulled on his trousers. Resumed his painful ascent of the hill of purgatory.

HILL OF PURGATORY. He laughed. Absurd really. But then this absurdity was consistent with the integrative, disintegrative functions of history, aggression, regression – location as well as dislocation. New/old world. Action of remorse. Prenatal configuration, postmortem fantasy, post-dynastic embassy. Sliding scale of living and dead representatives decked out in the crib as well as the coffin with the insignia of a dwarf of conscience. Crumb of the womb. Constitution of humility.

There was a poor village he knew on the Pomeroon (if one scanned the map of Guyana one might find it) named Charity. Another called Resurrection Bay where the natives begged bread of every passer-by.

There were the estates of a French landowner of the eighteenth century – La Penitence, Le Repentir (now the site of a cemetery in Georgetown) – all named by him to endorse a secret contract of remorse arising out of the death of his younger brother which he had unintentionally caused. He had flung a sharp stone in the heat of a game, a child's game, somewhere in France, which on striking his brother down arose afresh into the boot of exile, self-imposed exile, agency of fortune and conviction, traffic in slaves. Mid-Atlantic slate. Middle passage. Chalk of the Amazon. His last will and testament bequeathed a calculated sum to relieve the plight of orphans and turned the stone of death inside/out as it were. Dance of the muse. Dance of evolution. Sleepwalker of history. Saint and executioner of the orphanage. Reformation of the loop.

OH MY. Victor laughed like a man bereft of his wits yet sane as a clown. OMAI…

OH MY was a mushroom settlement far beneath the spectral watershed of Guyana, Amazon/Orinoco. Some said it was really OMAI – an Amerindian root word – subconscious foreboding. Others that a clown like Victor had invoked the substitution OH MY/OMAI. To forge a treaty of sensibility. English/Amerindian. Conqueror/Conquered. Free/Enslaved. Richman/Porknocker. Translation of the stigmata of the watershed. Was it a mirage of the senses, ruined faculty but therapeutic lighthouse, *opus contra naturam?*

OPUS CONTRA NATURAM. Victor stopped to read this inscription upon an outcrop of volcanic material – a peculiar intrusive lantern of geological age. It (stone and inscription) resembled sandstone, greenstone, auriferous constellation, igneous moon or painted Indian galaxy. Microcosmos of creation. Cradle of gloom. Tombstone of light. It emerged from the ground, or had fallen from the alphabet of the stars, riven and sculptured. Riven as by hellfire itself which it had once sustained like a lamp of the underworld. Sculptured as by the electricity of heaven which it had once held like the salt of nature… TIMEHRI – the aboriginal art of the jungle – which translated means THE HAND OF GOD…

Victor drew his hand in turn along the surfaces and crevices of this ancient memorial upon whose lantern skull (where the fire had blackened it) he thought he now discerned the slate of the ruined porknocker as a new ingrained element. The gold dusts, sandstones, sprinkled there had all been acquired, too, in their turn down the ages and could well have been a rainbow of chalks – lightning of grace. Precipitation as well as uprising.

In fact as Victor leaned upon the porknocker's tomb (Victor felt he could so name it since the slate of the porknocker was the latest grain of its alien body and reconstructive flying element) – leaned upon the enigma and epitaph *opus contra naturam* – he realized he had arrived at a sentry-box on the hill which afforded him a fantastic view of the misty chasm of the river. Precipitation as well as uprising. A kind of bird's eye view (radiant cannon) from the back of which – bird's mask, rainbow and arrow of nature – he was aware of himself as a transparent target, self-reversible bubble, siege of space, peacock's tail. Something native to the jungle. Native cannon. Aerial bombardment whose rays shone like ancestral splintered bullet. Rain of many colours. Arrow of blood. Implacable rebound. *It struck him now like a blow – mirage of the senses.* As if someone had crept up unawares and blinded him for an instant. Flung dust like slate upon cloud. Fading colours of the rainbow. Blood of the void. EYE OF THE VOID.

It dawned on him like pinpoint and stab that he was involved in a grotesque battle with the constable of the watershed, the ruined porknocker of space. And that the bombardment which he suffered (as protagonist or antagonist), mist or rain, gold or sand, sky or leaf, walking tree, slate or cloud was a meteoric flock flying through the eye of the void – implosive characteristic – even as it appeared to congeal or pause and encircle the tombstone of history like a radiant constellation, tail or fan. Victor felt he had gained his third illuminating milestone – first, boot of the clown (*bump on his forehead*), second, axe and ring (*scar on his neck*), third, wheel of the rainbow within slate or chalk (*eye of the void*). And that assailed as he was by light as well as dark, noon as well as night, beauty as well as pain – he could still discern (as if for the first time) a frail multiform conception of unity, terrestrial and transcendental…

He straightened up and began to climb again.

2

It was still early – coming up to an hour past noon – but Victor knew he had a long climb still before him. The trail he followed was forbidden, dangerous – sometimes straight up where a spoke or the gradient permitted it, sometimes around by exploiting the rim of the chasm. A trail which moved within humid and arid cycles of memory. FORBIDDEN CYCLES OF THE HEARTLAND. ANANCY TRAIL. RUINED PORKNOCKER. INVENTOR OF FRAMES. WELDER OF SEASONS. In the rainy season that now prevailed a great misty saddle arose from the chasm in his side like an archaic but fertile web, traffic of moistures, humidity's cycle.

But Victor was aware of an arid wheel as well; windbitten advertisement, the painted sun like a crude omnibus draped in cloud. DOUBLEDECKER OF THE UNIVERSE. As if sometimes the porknocker/inventor were his own illuminated carcass – salesman of the sky – territory which bounced his frame like rubber, dry stiff tyres of *pegasse* (which not even the moisture of the stars distilled like smoke could skid or undermine). A kind of fibrous shoe within or beneath the body of the hill, pneumatic fuel.

It was raining again and Victor drew little comfort from the glib assurances of the robot in his side, pneumatic fuel, ribbed watermarks, shoe of the hill. Skid or no skid he was entangled in an ancient web, forbidden net, dangerous adventure – psyche of history, stigmata of the void. He recalled the lines of a poem he had written (in another age it seemed) which he had destroyed long, long ago but which for some curious reason he now remembered as if it were the ghost of himself or he – the ghost of his poem. The lines, inadequate as they were, signified an obscure witness to the "first" sighting of Omai (mountain or cloud) – chasm of memory – OH MY CHASM – discovery of Atlantis (mythical America): Atlantic void, Pacific void, Roraima (lost world), Easter Island (lost men, brooding sculpture).

> "The longlost seas inundate his negative body, the
>   spiritual explorer
> by many shores of memory: the bright waves are
>   light
> like feathers upon his wide eyes.
>   Darkness falls in strange alarums
> like bells off San Salvador (music he heard in
>   imagination reached Columbus,
> was like a chorus of the dead
> reiterating old crimes for new discovery)
>   And sunset or sunrise
> was discovered equally guarding the mountain of his
>   heart."

The wind which arose struck him now to the marrow of his bones. Like a taste of snow. Peruvian snow. Watershed of the Amazon. He felt himself standing in a queue – queue of tears, frozen rain as it fell – waiting for the mocking blood of the elements to flow.

Melting trousers, *lacuna* of the watershed, a figure in the saddle of the hill, in the driving seat of rain…

Victor was becoming less and less certain of the trail. He could see the broad back of the hill against him now and that was all. His own feet as well as the other's were vanishing in time. A solid but mournful ridge of a head – lantern and clown of sky – still reached up from the tombstone of earth as if, were he (the chauffeur of the watershed) to turn and look back, his face would be encrusted with the omnibus he drove. Victor felt himself *pushed* in his frozen queue towards the wheel of carcass – *pushed… fall flat on his face.* The wheel enveloped him. Like a whirling glutinous blanket. Stung limbs – subterranean dawn.

WHEN HE AWOKE HE FELT THE CAKED SUN ON HIS BODY – WHEELS OF MUD – TYRE MARKS – MICROCOSMOS OF CRUCIFIXION, CREATION. The rain had ceased and the river in the chasm glittered. The tyre marks on his body dearly ran down into the chasm of the landscape – letters of psyche – sparkling wavelets – and up into the air – beads of oceanic moisture like scales and flakes – palimpsest and inscription – when an automobile, engine of climate, has passed.

CLIMATE OF ADVENTURE. It was the softness that beguiled him, yielding trail of premises, bodily/bodiless wheel, terrestrial/celestial spider, fingerprint/footfall of seasons. Rainfall. Rain-forest. Drought-savannah. Blanket of snow. Whirling aeroplane. North. South. East. West. OH MY CHASM. ADVENTURE OF SIN. APPETITE OF MILLIONAIRE. Zone to zone, geography of delirium. Had he been pushed or stung? BITTEN BY TARANTULA. OH MY GOD. Senses grown dim. Elongated. Telescope of pain. Faint pole to pole. Tripod of ice to tripod of fire. OH MY LEGS. GLOBAL FEVER. MAGNIFICATION OF PREMISES. TARANTULA.

Victor was aware of the escalation of a cross (tarantula glued to his eyes,) brushmarks of fever: wonders of science – spider's web printed upon the diaphragm of a telescope, collimation of frailty, identity, glass eye of science graduated to measure the globe, omnibus and address…

Global cross. Oath of humanity. As if he were indebted to a curse for alignment with the gods, the dreadful healing eye of the gods, mask of poison, therapeutic mystery, subsistence of memory, blanket and web.

"Mad to hope," Victor said to himself. "You're mad to

hope…" He steeled himself to draw blood, sliced into the poison of his leg. Mad to go on – *but must.* Must walk – dream to walk. Make to walk. Swore an oath – oath of humanity. He would pursue the ruined porknocker to the end of the world if need be.

From the fierce vantage point he now possessed, drenched in agony – edge of landfall, eye of science – the looming chasm of the river acquired an agility to scale mountains. Larger-than-life scale. Limbo dancer. Open-ended milestone. Empty tomb. Inversion and adjustment. Cross of the telescope. Collimation of waterfall. Ascending rather than descending. Wheel within a screw within a screw. *Spider transubstantiation. Trickster transubstantiation.* Metamorphosis of the Fall. *Deliverance and protection.*

The shock of inoculation (deliverance and protection), translation of the jaw of the spider, eye of the spider, into the omnibus of ascent, healing waterfall, imbued him with a brooding mirror and conception…

Kept his eyes glued… Inverting telescope. Recalled the inscription *opus contra naturam* on the ledge of the hill beneath him. Began with a telescopic nib (spider joint, anancy rib) to spin a reflective web or footnote which – by magnification – mirage of particulars – drew so close it almost brushed him.

"The disciple of history (*On this Rock I shall build…*) was crucified upside down to act as a warning that none, however privileged or gifted, may pretend to see with the psyche of history, Christ of history…"

Web. *Hubris.* "And therefore," he continued (anancy's tribe), "all we can hope to achieve through sickness and health, till death…" grimace of a clown… "is a re-assembly of that *caveat.* Mirror of humility. Void of conscription, *hiatus* of violence, door of origins. Revolution of the cross."

Felt his eyes fill with mineral tears, sandstone, earthstone, greenstone, rainbow, slate, sanctification of vacancy. Empty tomb.

The stratification of rock-epitaph he now appeared to possess (like an ingrained faculty, *camera obscura*) resembled (as in an abstract painting) a procession of witnesses, witnesses of the soul.

The first of these – teardrop of glass – shook and moved its location. Like a dewdrop, earring. Exquisite fossil. Magdalene of geology. It had taken ages of transference, evolution of fin, evolution of feather – ages of the riddle of lust – penetrations and modifications – to effect this chasm of daring, bridge of sight, bridge of sound, chasm of love. Coquette of God.. Coquette of the Sun. As though the chasm itself were a chameleon of longing within a mortal jealous colour and framework.

A bomb may have fallen and the hollow vessel of earth remaining enclosed itself like a single bead and mask. One eyed, one-eared globe. Its very transparency, its very hollowness, became the mystery of freedom, the mystery of indirection, reconstruction upon the brow of a formidable *caveat*.

He kissed her feet – the black Magdalene of earth – elongated pearl or toe of hollow ground where his lips stood. A shiver of ecstasy ran through him. Like a miser whose hoard of love – (division and multiplication of darkness-upon-darkness) – drew him to construct a curtain of fantasy. Mistress of wealth. Mistress of the globe. Mistress of the tomb.

The curtain parted upon a stage whereon his play SOUL was in progress. *Porknocker's Boudoir.* Theatre of Adventure.

Victor trained his encrusted eye. Geological and emotional tapestries. Tragedies. Million year old psyche. Curtains of comedy. War paint. Love paint. Black blonde resources. Blonde black milchcow. Negro. Indian. White.

He felt the humiliating burden of possession and dispossession: metallic loves, conscripted loves, threadbare loves – uncanny deprivations, manipulations – darkness-upon-darkness – light-upon-light – wholesale/retail crown – scalp or wig. Absurd mistress. Matriarchal advocate.

As if the Magdalene of Compassion saw him (Victor) for what he was, a bundle of nerves, ironic cradle of the soul, and drew a veil over his eyes, flesh upon a bald clown, skin over his bones, hair of protection – to repudiate an unfeeling yoke, confirm the subsistence of memory, mother of wisdom, cloak of memory, hearth and stone, shelter and mask, protective mission.

CHILD OF THE SPEAR

It was still early afternoon and the light upon the couch of the Magdalene curved like a spear. Rainswept hand of god. TIMEHRI. A child (Victor) was crying as the hallucinated spear flew and arched into the fourth milestone or door in his side. *Boot of stone.* Ring of bronze and iron. *Cannon of the void, rainbow of science.*

And now as the spear flew and arched Victor was aware of a time-lag of consciousness. Like a black opening kicked open by memory which were it to be filled by him with a concretization of violence would constitute an illusion. But were it to be accepted by him as a chasm of daring – would begin to convert the limbo of reflection into a spear of renewal. Spear in his side. Like a primitive abstraction, ritual fecundation of darkness-upon-darkness, milestone-within-milestone, where man becomes not only child again but god becomes man, shape-shifts, shape-changes, into his own vacant mother – the womb of mercy from which he had sprung…

Victor was three years old (DREAMT ON THE BRIDGE OF THE HILL) when the traumatic *caveat,* psychological shape-changing premises began. *A man and a woman were cohabiting on the floor.* Urban stomach – nightmare. Rotting boarding house. Single room. Congestion. Poverty. Art of the slums. Spectral intestines. Sometimes one elbow to a family of ten. He could see them clearly (or was it confusedly): the chasm of her thighs. A cloud like trousers draped over rock.

Victor cried. The man reached up. Drunk father of ages. Veiled form on the other side of the globe. Gave him a clout: inside. "BUGGER THE CHILD OF AGES," he whispered and cried. "QUIET. PLEASE." Poked him in the side: inside. Spear of the clown. *Dreamt of them now as if he were inside, still waiting to be born, on the other side of the globe, inside the man, inside the woman.* Misty figures. Shape-changing. Shape-shifting. Leaps and bounds. Spectral flesh. Grotesque clown. Limbo side, spear in his side. Like a phantom dancer under a milestone, limbo dancer, cross and spear, arched door.

Never knew his mother. Died when he was born. A voluminous petticoat hanging on the wall was all that remained to speak of her. Subsistence of memory. Victor curled himself up there, protective skin, memory's dress. His father was drunk. Boxing Day. The room was a shambles. Victor remained hidden there (within the petticoat) until it was safe to emerge: crawled on the floor towards a window. Twentieth century window. It was raining outside. Raining blood. Global civil war. Insurrection Day. He could hear the drums on the road – lightning and thunder – the rowdy band of Albuoystown. He pulled himself up – *there they were:* rowdy elements, descendants of "free" men and "slaves". Apochrypha of the living and the dead. Insurrection womb and race. Dance of ironical victor and victim. Strong ageless women dancing on stilts in waistcoat and trousers (high up – off the ground – in the sky); and great limbo men in striped drawers and dresses sliding under a bar. Limbo bar. Inverse location of sex. Door of rebirth. Sanctification of otherness.

Sanctification of grotesquerie. Porknocker's race. His father was a compulsive dancer, troublemaker, fighter (member of the rowdy band himself), compulsive miner (combed the Cuyuni for gold) but since the death of his wife – Victor's mother – had become stone-drunk, crazed by grief, and had returned to his original craft – welding. His sole ambition now was to build his own shop, working premises. Set up as a capitalist. Make war on poverty. The odds were against him since his was a poorly paid profession – a dog's life – part and parcel of an illegitimate technology, metallurgical brood, foundry and fire.

Sometimes when he returned from the factory in Albuoystown (a miserable week's pay in his pockets), blackened overall, he looked like hell and ambition making love in the same bed. Where else in fact could they lie if he were to bugger the metal of ages. Burn the factory of ages. Poor Adam. Ultimatum of heaven. Usually he squandered the few pennies he might have saved on a woman he brought in with him from the streets.

Victor would hide beneath the petticoat of his ancient mother and keep his eyes glued through its misty fabric upon the living copulation of the dead. Numb with the day's fatigue, fascination and misery. Stone-drunk father and stony-eyed mistress. AS IF ON THE OTHER SIDE OF THE CURTAIN WHERE HE LAY FORTY YEARS LATER HE WAS AWARE OF THE DANGER OF FALLING A VICTIM TO A MESMERISED QUEUE-CHILD-IN-THE-WOMB, WOMB-IN-THE-CHILD-LOVE AND HATE, WAR AND INDUSTRY ROLLED INTO ONE: STAGE-CARPENTER, WELDER OF RIBS, JACK-OF-ALL-TRADES, INVENTOR OF THE NUDE MIRROR. A CURSE AND A BLESSING ROLLED INTO ONE.

Victor felt as he studied the legend of his father, fresh from slavery, fresh from the factory, rum-soaked labour (Boxing Day overtime) that here was the masked creator of Insurrection Day long before the Russian Revolution, Lenin or Trotsky, Stalin or Devil. He was stung, ashamed, by a burning odour, guilt of emotion, precipice of emotion. His father was the yoke shared by all of the sacred and profane (Christmas Day/Boxing Day/Insurrection Day) and he (Victor) felt his eyes being welded too, soldered too by frustrated divinities (copulation of idols – Africa, Asia, Europe) so that as the dancers swept by on the holiday street-shape-changing, shape-shifting in a dream – he perceived them through a veil of profanity, a veil of sanctity, man/ woman, holiday/holy day, father/mother...

The voluminous hill or coat to which he clung, sanctification of motherhood, intercession of motherhood, turned to limbo in his side: mirror in his side: whose exploding venom coiled around him like magnesium – acid flame, blue lightning, welder's mask, visor and tool, tarantula. He felt the rain of limbo seep through the window to his soul, chasm of her thighs, like a weakening of the penalty of fire. Blanket of lightning, elemental plague of mercy, dance of mercy, dance of compassion.

3

Victor secured a scholarship at the age of ten which took him straightaway to the best day school in the land. A phenomenally precocious but also phenomenally unprepossessing child. Came from a poor home – La Penitence and Albuoystown. Wore a large hat (globe of a head, rings of hair); red eyes, white mouth – hunger and solder. Tin soldier of fortune. Painted black. STAGE INSTRUCTIONS AS FOLLOWS: *Dip in fire. Plunge in water. Make for all seasons, weathers, rain, sun. Manufacturers. El Dorado.*

Victor laughed. I'm a funny guy (he said to himself apologetically). One day I shall be great, great and funny. How absurd. Maybe that's what great guys really are – *funny.*

His body was thin. He felt that if he could see himself walking in the distance he would look like a stick, comical outcast (league boots, mandatory premises – too large for his feet), mascot, dancer, globetrotter. All on one leg.

His unorthodox globe possessed many dimensions, many rooms (Africa, Europe, Asia) all, however, unfurnished: spun web, vacant ancestors, slum clearance, limbo traffic. His mother became an immortal. Immortal absence, embrace, bed of longing upon which he lay face down sometimes in the tropical afternoons, a voluminous housecoat beneath which he hid when his father was drunk and it was raining and he could not escape out of doors.

Sometimes his immortal mother was a tree against which

he propped himself, head in a book, feet upraised on trunk, crucifixion, cloud. *On this Rock I shall build…*

Sometimes a deserted corner in a field, a mound of grass, tombstone.

Thus it was – sheltered by the various over-arching premises of the womb of mercy – he saw the furies of history go by: John Gabriel Stedman's terrifying account of atrocities inflicted by Europeans upon Revolted Negroes in the Guianas (engravings by Blake, Blake the visionary whom he loved and admired and whom he identified with Old/New Testament, with Prophecy).

Tyger, tyger, burning bright
In the forests of the night…

Furies recounted too by earlier still colonisers (Portuguese and Spanish), conquistadors – gold-rush fiends, abnormal appetite for fame and fortune. At such moments an enlargement of his own spoil of memory enveloped him. The sun burnt a hole in his side. His father's copulations grew titanic. Titan of longing, conqueror and conquered…

A blade of grass pricked him. He plucked it, chewed it like a rag – daydream – pillow, green flag, cradle (porknocker's barrel floating in cloud, oceanic tub, ailing subsistence, middle passage).

At such an impressionable age – weaned on *vacancy* as well as *magnification,* inflation as well as deflation of disasters – every stroke of the cane (one, two, three, four, five, six, seven, eight, Down sir! Down dog! Boys must not be late – schoolmaster's cane) became an additional nail in his cross: comic cross, comic bastard, bunk of empire, cat-o'-nine tails, auction block. Was he a mascot for sale, after all, global sale, mascot of survival, exhibition scholar? His tutors meant to exploit him to the limit, rack him for his own good, send him to the top of the class. He was a find, a child-prodigy, monster. This haunted backside – irreverence in the face of instruction and chastisement – drew a callous spirit around him (hardened muse rather than actual monster). An unblushing metaphysic. Black feet in the sun. Crucifixion of Peter. So that at the stroke of eight – hellfire schoolmaster, brimstone angel – the mist of pain revolved into unfurnished subject rather than hated master…

Had it not been for the sanctification of vacancy, footsteps in the wind, limbo dancer, he would have succumbed to a brutal concretization of the ghostly cane – gross material "saviour" or gross material "devil"…

Whereas the spear in his side, OH MY CHASM, sanctification of dream, began to create its own revolving wheel of compassion, self-created capital, ironic counterpoint, fecundation of darkness-upon-darkness, light-upon-light…

4

THEATRE OF BREAD

Victor wrote stage instructions on a leaf of his exercise book as follows (he laughed with relish): *Train mirror. Shine quickly into eyes of approaching father or enemy (identity unknown). Make him stumble. Limbo dancer.*

To begin with – early in the year – afternoons – he lay in wait in an alleyway near the foundry with his mirror snug in his side to catch the sun and turn it full, dazzling, bright, upon his father's countenance. His father brushed – furiously, irritably – at spider or bread. Always the first to emerge (Victor knew) – stable of the underground – in the procession from oven and factory. Face when the mirror struck looked pasty, wild: carnival paste, metamorphosis, lightning horse, eyes plastered, plugged, prizemoney, bread.

Victor chewed, swallowed – sixpence for dinner and supper. Chewed again. Inadvertently bit his tongue: tasted like tin – sixpence and bread. Hated his father; idolized him. Bread. Sixpence of idolatry. Prayer of idolatry.

Prayed to his idol to give him bread: bread he needed to fill his side, gnawing side, gnawing appetite, tin mines, silver mines, gold mines, OH MY CHASM; appetite for emotion, appetite for knowledge, appetite for industry. Growing side, growing lust, growing persuasion. Prayed to his father-idol to give him bread, daily bronze, daily bread, coal, copper, rock, sand, rust, furnace, OH MY BREAD.

If only his father would hear his prayer and furnish him with bread, furnish the millionaire rooms in his side – he would fall down *now* in the alleyway of the foundry: worship him. Furniture of Chasm. Omai Chasm. Bake him, melt him, stew him, sculpt him, worship him.

It was his unfurnished chasm after all – chasm of millionaire. Why not? Hated his father for being poor. Idolized him – fantasy of wealth – breadwinner (racehorse of the sun) – porknocker's stable.

As the year advanced his trained mirror worked no longer in the alleyway near the foundry. Instead he ensconced himself on a fence which ran along St. Saviour's Churchyard. Here he found once again he could catch the sun and speed the light into his father's eyes. Where there had been bread before there was now curry. Promotion at the foundry. Ninepence for supper. Rod and curry. The stable door clanged – factory door – door of the tomb. His father's eyes (blinded by the mirror of the sun) were dripping molten copper.

As the year still advanced he climbed yet higher in the afternoon towards sunset, weaving a web of gold, mirror in his side; sometimes like standing water, wide and full, reflection of joy: sometimes like an iron cloud, dark *clang* shut in his side, self-exile. First there had been the alleyway of bread (tin mine); then a state of curry (copper mine). Now in order to retain the right conjunction (father and sun) he needed to ascend and move around higher still.

There was an old wall running around a disused warehouse – much higher than the fence of St. Saviour's Churchyard. This would afford him anew the angle and coincidence he needed – an hour or so before sunset – metamorphosis of metals.

It gave him (as he waited for his father to come) a view of the river, white, beaten gold at first, turning magnificently and slowly into scarlet lion, bronze child, cloud, sailing vessel, fishing craft, rocking tub under a feather. A whale of a steamer began to appear – doubledecker of sunset. Still no sign of his father.

Who knows (Victor dreamt) – he may have been transferred there, for a day or two, on that whale of an anchor. An expert welding job. Bauxite money. Aluminium. Fish to melt in his mouth. Overtime. Victor wondered whether one day he would own not only racehorses but bauxite plants in Demerara, aluminium processing factories in Canada. Atlantic ferry. Fleet of buses. Own it as if it were light as a feather. Gossamer scale. Petticoat made of butter. Bullet made of security. Self-ironical light, theatre of bread, sunset, porknocker's boudoir. *Still no sign of his father.*

Victor felt curiously alarmed. There had been talk for weeks now of a general strike which would involve the factory. *No sign of his father, stable of the underground.* It had come – yes – he felt it in his bones – the Strike…

It would mean (he cursed softly) once again tightening his belt. His allowance had been increased – bread and meat – overtime. But with a strike everything would go back to starvation level. He was torn – hatred and idolatry. Hatred of the factory. STRIKE, YES, WHY NOT? Idolatry of bread, idolatry of meat, idolatry of capital. STRIKE, NO, NOT NOW.

He could hear voices at the bottom of the chasm, then a single voice it seemed talking back and forth, talking to him, rubbing it in. Self-absorption. He had been caned that day in school for burning a hole in his exercise book. Heat of the sun. Blazing mirror. "Daylight robbery," schoolmaster and judge had said. "Taxpayers' money."

"Twelve strokes with the cat," the voice in the chasm intoned. "Man of brimstone. Sentenced by the court."

Victor felt accused, accursed, humiliated, embarrassed. Embarrassed and humiliated by nightmare robot he had been inclined to take for granted, unfurnished cane, unfeeling yoke (master and slave). As if the ironic counterpoint which had been a source of emancipation before, vacant millions, had begun to sear him to the bone. He remembered.

ON THE HILL WHERE HE LAY FORTY YEARS LATER THE STRIKE BEGAN TO RETURN. SIX MONTHS OF STRIKE. BURNING OF FACTORY BY HIS FATHER OR FATHER'S MATE. SENTENCED TO THE CAT. SEVEN YEARS' HARD LABOUR.

Brimstone had been his father's mirror, father's shadow. Sat side by side on the same bench... factory. Close friends from far back, schooldays. Same name, same build. *Adam.* Some people were confused when sentence was passed – were they one and the same... shadow... mate... conscience?

Dubbed a mysteryman, cane-breaker at school... hard ass ... workbench. Lost his hide, job. Lost his scholarship (Victor's imagination moved in concert now with the robot in his side – robot prisoner, robot millions).

BOOK II

ASCENT

Since the dead are concerned with the living, the initiative for communication comes as often from them as from their descendants. This is no inert debris of vanished cultures but a dynamic source of energy seeking for release and which, failing to find it through creative communion, may spend itself in thunderbolts and convulsions of nature.

GERALD MOORE (*The Chosen Tongue*)

5

The events of his life when sentence was passed seemed now to him both glaring and obscure. He contracted malaria.

Quinine. Sometimes three tablets a day. Fifteen grains in all. In between bouts of fever an enormous clarity descended: a *deaf* clarity (there was no other way of describing it – quinine made one deaf) as though in some hallucinated manner his ears were cemented in pavement, wood, slate, aluminium, in the furniture of the world, the world of things, theatre of the robot.

And he saw these – the objects around him – so unemotionally and lucidly that a strange *hubris* overtook him: an assumption of painless comedy enacted everywhere – the crucifixion of the robot. A roof, after all, which had been stitched with planks, convicts' muscle, was nothing but a roof (he reasoned); a stone, after all, which had been quarried and broken, convicts' lungs, nothing but a stone; a tree, after all, which had been twisted and bent, convicts' fantasy, nothing but a tree; flesh, after all, which had been furred and torn, convicts' cat, nothing but flesh. Nerveless identity. It was all so lucid, so abstract, drained of superstition (cinematic menu, euthanasia of the absurd, consuming appetite of the dead) that he dreamt he had emancipated the "object" – overthrown the seal of pain…

This was the prison of reality (or irreality) in which Adam dwelt. Futuristic robot. Ruined porknocker. Insensible soul, insensible insurrection, insensible bone, insensible nerve. It was as if he had already ceased to exist and Victor's journey in search of him possessed an order of fatality – "immaterial" adventure of the soul, *opus contra naturam.*

As if the sentence passed on him had been one of extinction – extinction of species – extinction of tribes. As if the trial itself – the trial he had endured – had never happened or ceased to exist beyond its grossest material forms (hated devil, crude saviour) in becoming the decimation of past idols (decimated saviour/devil, master/pupil, judge/judged, boot/brow, axe/neck…).

As if the placards the processions of welders once carried – processions of sunset – were desensitized even as they read TYGER, TYGER, BURNING BRIGHT (as they faced the dying primitive sun, appetite for fire), devoid of pain even as they declared CRUCIFIXION OF BREAD, COMEDY OF BREAD (as they faced the Alleyway of Tin, appetite for wealth), devoid of suffering even as they cried CRUCIFIXION OF MEAT, DEVALU-ATION OF COPPER (as they faced St. Saviour's Churchyard, appetite for God). As if it were all a gigantic hoax – the antithesis of gross material idolatry and yet the confirmation of idols (gross nail, atom).

As if the pickets around the factory were inherently voice-less and the fire of Eden, claustrophobic Eden, a blind for all ages.

As such – by a curious almost diabolical regression of the instincts – the total nature of things *grieved* to extend itself into a courtroom of truth – a drama of soul – myth as well as man – stigmata of the void. A courtroom as large and painful as the globe in Victor's head and as subjective as the mirror of appetite in his side.

Victor perceived in the new courtroom OH MY that Adam himself was not there – could not (in the very circumstances of *hubris* and incarceration) be "present". Unless one learnt to root him out from his *malaise,* euthanasia of the absurd…

"My mother," Victor recalled with a sudden jolt – "fulfilled this craving in me for immortal *hubris*... Poor tree, vacant petticoat. Poor mother..."

As if a curious compassionate irony prevailed – and yet a kind of shamanistic sabotage in which father became mother and Eden burning in their sides turned into the strike of the womb, clinical joke, lifeless shell.

The courtroom then – in its extension and regression – trial of the soul – was the birth of a new ultimate drama, ultimate questions (end-of-globe adventure?).

As if the mirror of the sun stood in such intimate juxtaposition to centuries of depression, the decimation of Aboriginal and conquered peoples (Carib, Arawak, Pole, Arab, Negro, Jew, Irish, Hungarian, countless others) that it shared the ghost of the womb. It was equally the Styx of pride – robot emancipation, robot fascination, curtain of relief – as it was the candle of dawn, mystery tale, chasm of dreams, father/mother candle, child/parent sun, self recreative summit and psyche.

As the trial reopened in his side the indictment of sabotage re-framed itself into a comedy of the soul... gestation of the soul.

As though the genealogy of an age, judge and judged, master and pupil, man and world, patent of the law, poet and craftsman, were equally in the dock. And the dock was everywhere, robot springs, bicycle and automobile, omnibus and aeroplane, spectral watershed, *circumambulatio,* sun's movement around the earth (as ancients believed), earth's revolution around the sun (as moderns calculate).

The first witnesses to come forward were Alias Tin (born in Alleyway of Bread), Alias Copper (born in St. Saviour's Churchyard), Alias Wall (born overlooking the river), Alias Picket (born in Albuoystown diametrically opposite Alleyway of Bread). All sprung equally from the spear in his side which Victor focused upon the queue of the underground in his circular path with the skin of the sun around the door of stage and school, prison and factory. As such their parentage was devious, cunning and wry – an inner cross rather than a faceless unfelt composition.

6

Victor resumed his ascent to Omai. The afternoon had cleared
somewhat. The drone of an aeroplane arose to the south. At
first he saw nothing. Then a glimmer shone in the sky like a
crumb of glass. Flashed in his eye as if it shone across porknocker
miles, welded *time – from his gaoled hands in Albuoystown* – deity
and child – reflected now in space. So that in a sense he had
become in forty years his own constellated mirror shining
now *from* him (as if he were up there in the sky) and *upon* him
(as if he were down here in his father's shoes).

Victor began to consider closely the nature of his father's
trial which now obsessed him. He knew now it wasn't simply
a question of schizophrenic identity. It was, in fact, a profound
bitter question of confronting the legacies of the past in which
he and all men were involved through parent or friend,
employer or employed; trader or trade, captor or captive, etc.,
etc. These legacies – extending into time and eternity – could
assume all sorts of proportions, apparently *unfeeling* raw material as well as apparently *feeling* unity. But the truth was one had
to confront it all – whether through loss or gain – with the
greatest care if one were not to succumb to self-deception. It
was – amongst other things – a question of continuously
revising one's conception of function, of re-considering, so to
speak, the origin of function within a variety of signals and
complexes.

It was important, Victor realized, to sift the ground of

obsession upon which and within which one moved. What an extraordinary illusion it was, for example, to conceive of himself in his father's shoes and to feel upon his own brow, as it were, the flashing mirror he had himself exercised out of hate and love for his parents, absent mother (petticoat) and welder-father. As if somewhere there in space, over the years of subsistence, the energy he had stored as a child each time he flashed the light on his father's brow on his way to or from school possessed both psychic and technological features that were bound to return from the depths and heights of proliferate nature. It was as though each time he flashed the mirror he was relaying a series of ghosts that were born of his own unconscious reserves (past and future) within which lived a series of mirrors at various removes in time and eternity. Those unconscious or unfeeling reserves appeared to occupy a technological station when the mirror in his hand and the light of the sun seemed nothing more than the raw material of the moment. But actually that raw material carried within it, so to speak, relative areas of feeling – deeper and deeper urgencies or higher and higher omens of reflection.

To put it in one way – the mirror of forty years ago through which he poured the light of attack upon his father who stood in the door of the factory became the constellated hands of OH MY flashing now back as if he were the inventor or creator of his father's ghost. Inventor or creator of a fortress of conscience just as he had invented or created within his mother's housecoat a fortress of love in time of distress.

Victor was only too well aware how precarious these establishments were – precarious but enduring because *something* continuously remained to subsist on the reversible, convertible body of the present like a series of ghosts psychic in that they deepened the emotions and feelings – technological in that they constellated themselves within a crumb of glass like a pinprick of milk upon his mother's breast in space, needle's eye of sweat upon his father's brow in space, wing-tip or bone, petticoat, housecoat, vanishing aeroplane.

As the mirror of the sun translated him – endowed him with a star of memory – crumb of glass – ancient childlike dress (welded cloud) – Victor grew aware of Alias Tin in the gloom of the forest. He (Victor) had arrived in his ascent of the hill at a subsidiary watershed which branched away like a handlebar or ridge. Had it not been for the aeroplane's wing-tip, glistening on OH MY like dust or milk, cloth or food, he would have missed the conversion or glimmer upon Alias Tin who stood forty yards from the wheel of the chasm like nature's ghost. Like tinned blood, rust and grain, manna of space.

Victor stopped – *blood* – No. Alias Tin was bloodless. And yet as Victor's eye caught the light of the sky it was as if – from the distant winged past and winging future – within a series of ghosts constituting the breadwinner of space – he perceived blood cascading through the trees like the sublimation of a waterfall, ghost of nature, ghost of OH MY/ OMAI, ghost of the ridge, constable of the watershed. A strange holy/unholy compound it was reflected there dressed in a meteor, clown of divinity, idol of humanity: claim of bloodlessness: claim of blood.

It stood (he observed) – this witness of sensibility and insensibility – within the door of the forest like the poverty of all creation, star of all invention, Adam's pole upon which a ruined fabric of aeroplane had been nailed like an epitaph, flesh or flag, fornication of space. Here, in fact, Adam had first come and settled with a woman upon his release from prison. He had staked a mining claim here after stumbling through what looked like the wreckage of his own factory – the one he had burnt down – but which was actually a shattered aircraft that had crashed on Omai ridge a year or two ago. For all the world now like the dispersal of himself – timeless and listless calendar – ghost of everyman's trail, ghost of evolution.

He had salvaged a piece of tin for a headboard or witness to his claim since this had to be erected, according to law, to ensure his prospecting rights. It was now all overgrown with fern Victor saw like tarantula, masked fabric or aircraft on which had been inscribed – MINING CLAIM TAKEN BY ONE ADAM, MANNA OF SPACE, THIS CENTURY OF GHOSTS, TWENTIETH CENTURY. (It was the habit of pork-nockers to christen their claims with idiosyncratic relish compounded nevertheless of curious irony and compassion).

As Victor crawled through the undergrowth into the claim, the obsessive robot of memory stung him afresh. His head almost touched the ground like a limbo dancer – one of those fantastic performers he remembered seeing as a child in Albuoystown on holidays dancing under a horizontal pole through what seemed the keyhole of space. As if they belonged to a limbo fortress in which they moved plastic as dough, subtle as fish, fluid and stinging as currie; and through which Victor broke now as from the seal he had himself planted there long ago on his father's eyes like the ghost of subsistence, fortress of subsistence. Thus it was again he was confronted by psychic/technological features – rather, in this instance, by psychic/dramatic features wherein the dance of the soul expressed itself through latent formations of appetite and memory, expression and mood, agility and rigidity, vertical pole, horizontal couch, wheel and spin, limbo aircraft.

Victor felt the strangest *rapport* now as he crawled on the ground between Adam and the ruined pilot and crew of Omai. A *rapport* extending, he felt, out of the dance of limbo – rowdy band of the elements in Albuoystown. "OMAI CHRIST, OMAI MAGDALENE," he cried to the Bush. Thus it was – long after the fire and the crash – he found himself touched by his own holy/unholy lightning reserves to pray for the living and the dead community everywhere (convertible body of humanity) toppling through a crack in the earth or ceiling of cloud, ceiling of eternity equally in space as time, thirty thousand feet up on the ridge of Omai, thirty thousand years down in the chasm of OH MY.

It was the most curious door of memory in the fortress of limbo Victor unlocked as he investigated his father's claim. The earth over which he moved gently and carefully like a puppet of prayer was cracked since the intermittent rain falling that day and seeping here earlier had not yet repaired the signs of a drought. There were glimmers of sun too like electric light stored in the ruined body of the bush as though at one time the Bush itself had been on psychic fire, lit by Moses, an ancient revered porknocker, and now what remained was the ruination of that true prophetic mirror of legend and history. Victor was conscious that the *rapport* Adam had established with the crashed pilot whose wing-tip adorned the head of his claim in the shape of Alias Tin was of enormous significance in providing the, fortress of limbo with both curvature and density.

Victor himself was aware of his own susceptibility to the puppetry of limbo (serial ghost, curvature of limbo) and, in fact, it was this confession that provided him with a peculiar new self awareness he had never known quite in that way before. In his journey to Omai across the jungle and his ascent to OH MY above the jungle he had been stung, kicked, beaten by the subtle as well as crude weapons of nature and society into hypnosis. A hypnosis which provided him with what would have been a comic duality of function if he were not himself convinced that that duality was the twin apparition of death. It was this twin ghost that terrified him at first since it seemed but the duplication of his own mortal wound transferred into space, nailed to the sky, constellated in the density as well as extrapolative mirror of origins. But now later (after the first flush of terror) that duplication of the mortal trap appeared to him an illusion. Perhaps a necessary *conviction* at one stage of his ascent.

The fact was it was the repudiation of the robot – of the puppet – which was actually at stake all the time through a revelation of itself as a ruined instrument of *unruined* consciousness, as a brain that was instrumental rather than ultimate. A revelation of unruined consciousness that went to the heart of the human brain or hell on earth by, as it were, *persisting* through and within all ruined personality, like a salutary lighthouse within and beyond desolation or claim, fortress or wall.

Victor felt himself now immersed in the ground of *rapport* between Adam and the ruined pilot of the aeroplane. He felt himself a passenger in a waiting-room whose brain ceases to function (hypnotic disembodiment) as he is about to board his aircraft – ceases to perform its ritual function – so that an illuminating equation emerges between the coming crash of the vehicle and his (the passenger's) normally suppressed lightning of emotion. He finds himself stricken in advance by an equation of frustration – omen or warning – radar ghost *before* and *after* the crash and he feels now that if he should travel on this vehicle he is already a "dead" man. . . . Was this pre-configurative disaster (Victor asked Alias Tin) similar to Adam's post-configurative digestion – twin apparition of death – ultimate repudiation of robot? YES, said Tin.

But Victor knew he was a long way still from being satisfied by a simple affirmation of eternity. A long way still to climb to sift the reality of *feeling* from *unfeeling* cloak of emancipation or industry. There was, first of all, an important question he must endeavour to answer. Had he been the passenger in the waiting-room about to board his plane would he have had the naive courage (or cowardice), common sense (or uncommon sense) to abandon his flight – in the face of official remonstrances, threats of forfeiting his air-fare, etc. – all because of a momentary hypnotic intuition?

Or – take it another way – if that intuition persisted like a drug might he not have been content to remain knowledgeable of the coming crash – like a kind of super-official mask – and yet indifferent to the consequences?

Or – take it still again in another way – might he not have enjoyed the sensation of knowing the plane was already empty and all who sat in it were, in fact, akin to a technological mirage on the threshold of conflagrative identity?

Ghost aircraft in short. One often saw them in deserted hangars like derelict evolutionary premises, naked and forlorn.

So that sentence having been passed in the very entrenched nature of things, wherein then lay the possibility of parole, genuine parole, true parole from the whole forlorn prison-house of adventure, claim of Adam, backside of the moon, OH MY?

Now (Victor confessed to Pilot Tin) he was jumping the gun. Why speak of parole (seven years or forty) when judge and jury had not yet been defined?

Take first the judge. VICTOR LEANED BACK IN THE TOMB OF SPACE AS HE VISUALIZED HIS HYPOTHETICAL KNOWL-EDGEABLE PASSENGER SPEEDING TO CRASH IN AN HOUR OR TWO IN A STORM ON OMAI.

There he (Alias judge, Alias Victor) sat for all the world as if he knew his goose had been cooked, done to a turn, slightly add (tin), slightly venomous like a fossil cigar (mildew, ver-tiginous gold) – dish of evolution. No shivers or gooseflesh as one might think: merely a kind of pucker or grin under his shirt where the whips of memory began to cut, secretly, subjectively, cat-o-nine tails, cat of god, cooked to a turn.

It was as if (Victor marvelled) this collective passenger, embodying pilot and crew, in the hour before his death, anticipated not only the scarred ridge of OH MY/OMAI where he would crash but the poor felon and creature (Victor's father) who would arrive there a year or two later to stumble upon the wreckage of his own past, ruined Eden, bed and board. Thus the stigmata of parole (Adam's parole) rose on the judge's back (Alias Victor, Alias Pilot, Alias Crew) within an hour of his death.

Victor now saw that the judge sitting there was himself –

cheek pressed to velvet glove and upholstery of the aircraft. He (Victor) toyed now with a writing-pad upon which he drew the outline of a novel history (his father's trial) through the witnesses he (the judge) had interrogated forty years ago. For the curious thing was the judge felt an irreality within himself, a vacancy or lack of self-definition – so to speak – which was so profound it became native to the prisoner at the bar as well, the prisoner of memory. *Why, in God's name, had the poor man run berserk and burnt factory as well as bed and board?* It was a question he scribbled on his pad away from the eyes of the jury and other officials of the court. Scribbled on the aeroplane flying to OH MY. And since he remained helpless after all these years, in defining the prisoner as in defining himself, the best course open to him now, in the last hour or two of his life, was to uncover the stubborn reality of the witnesses – those so-called witnesses on whom the weight of office, judge or jury, did not rest, and who were in a position to enjoy the scene in a critical or pseudo-critical manner since, in effect, they believed they were not themselves on trial and thus immune to penalty: therefore in a self-congratulatory position like guests in a large, well-appointed, kitchen surveying the oven and smacking their lips inwardly with hellish glee or heavenly disdain.

It was these witnesses enshrouded in an illusion of glee or wit or poetry or disdain whom the judge wished to uncover before his death on Omai.

For the truth was since he felt himself and the prisoner now truly in the same abnormal ill-defined dock, it became clear to him how subversive such a feeling was, half-suicidal even, half-consenting to doom like Mayakovsky's cloud in trousers. And therefore if he were to lay hold of what was really real about himself in this crisis he must uncover the witnesses of the unfeeling past – their graven solidity and convention of stature. If this seemed harsh, blunt, regressive to a body of tyrannous instinct, one must bear in mind – the judge mused

– that there was bound to be a nostalgic yearning for security and order in anyone, any representative (of an institution) like himself (whether law or empire, East or West) who felt himself on the threshold of breakdown or collapse.

It was human after all that a ruined identity such as his, involved in projecting itself into the future as a medium of justice or truth, would weigh both

(a) the intuitions of ghostly conscience, serial ghosts, Eumenides of conflict *before* and *after* the blast of an age (through the crash of an age); and

(b) the graven witnesses remaining to it whose immunity to penalty or punishment might prove the greater mystery after all – the true implacable fortress of the law.

Take, for example, in order to hang on to sublime immunity in the face of ridiculous penalty – the judge could not help nursing his humours – the clear soup the hostess of the aircraft had brought him. It glimmered under his nose with a trace of vegetable. He started eating (he was hungry), caught himself still smoking, stubbed out his cigar. What foul absentmindedness! How could one dream to eat soup and consume, at the same time, such a filthy weed? For the pleasure, no doubt, of catching oneself out as a kind of monster whose share in the prisoner at the bar, the prisoner of memory, lay not through an ordeal of compassion but through moral wit, breeding, recipes of insulation, civic duty. If he were a spokesman of the Philistines he would be drawn to shape a cynical line or two with economy and deliberation – make it materially binding upon posterity: exquisite fortress: exquisite moral of death whose callous appetite he confirmed as the true governing witness of discrete participation at the heart of life.

The judge was drawn to look away from his soup and through the window of the aeroplane. He was flying over a kind of plateau. And from this height – thirty thousand feet up in space – the earth glistened like a crab on whose back lay the stripes of the cat, stigmata of the void. The peculiar metaphor of evolution (geological suns as well as primitive cross) drew him back to reconsider the fortress on his pad. Soup and cigar. Crab and tiger. Were they indeed the infinite callousness of the graven appetite of time – infinite self-cannibal – or did they constitute an omen of grace after all, infinite shroud of mankind, mordant wit, stomach and courage, masks and manners, to stave off a gnawing limitation of the senses, an uncomfortable region within the cloak of Philistine, creator and inventor, judge and judged, physician and patient?

"Yes," said the judge, "perhaps that's why I stayed on the aircraft. I am the Philistine of OH MY. It's a question of the uncomfortable region one must approach time after time, again and again, down the ages shrouded by death in order to learn to bear by degrees what would otherwise be quite clearly (as my witnesses testify) unbearable: the classical truths of courage and compassion which are the stuff, sometimes, of the greatest poetry.

> Whilst my Physicians by their love are grown
> Cosmographers, and I their Mapp, who lie
> Flat on this bed, that by them may be shown
> That this is my South-west discoverie
> *Per fretum febris,* by these streights to die,
> I joy, that in these straits, I see my West;
> For, though theire currants yeeld returne to none,
> What shall my West hurt me? As West and East
> In all flatt Maps (and I am one) are one,
> So death doth touch the Resurrection."

The judge puckered his lips slightly as he spoke the last line to himself. Far up in a mist of light – with the earth like a glaze or map beneath him – he was only too well aware of the strange fascination of the poem embodying nevertheless (within the treacherous bounty and consolidation of genius) a temptation to succumb to mathematics of euphoria as the guide-lines of commonwealth.

In an hour or two he calculated it would be sunset, sunset of his life. Down below on the ground, already, across the immense backbone of the Americas, the sun may already have set for some.

He scribbled on his pad something he recalled from Disselhoff and Linné – "Anthropomorphic lidded urns used in secondary burials are distributed over a wide area of the Amazon lowlands, extending northwards as far as Venezuela and the Guianas."

The judge pondered the novel history he had begun to write. Would it ever see the true light of day? Here, far up in space, with the enormous advantage of increased curvature, the horizon would soon be intensely aglow as if, in fact, on a margin of earth, one had set the clock back to an earlier projection (in order to gain at least an hour's grace, an hour's extra light) whereas straight overhead one had set the clock forward to a later projection (in order to gain the crown of night and a housecoat of stars in conjunction with the mirror of the sun).

Mathematics of euphoria, the judge mused, was one way perhaps of describing it (think of the enormous residue of empires, pre-Columbian, post-Columbian) but clearly, within the complex wreckage of adventure and establishment, was something innately and profoundly architectural, to grasp which was, the judge felt, part of the hypnotic compulsion drawing him to Omai.

For the first time in his life he felt he was in process of weighing a certain balance of natures –

(a) the graven witness of light and darkness and their curvature of participation (compounded neither of penalty nor punishment);

    (b) the disembodied ghosts of time flying in anticipation
and reality *before* and *after,* below and above the aircraft.

In a curious way it was also possible to reverse the material/
immaterial function of the court and assume the graven
witness of night and day flew before and after the aircraft like
a reflection of intangibles whereas the serial ghost it was who
compounded a discrete affirmation.

It was here, in fact, within the "lost" architecture of memory
that the quest for OH MY assumed all the hazards of pitiless
divorce from origins as well as pitiful vacancy – alien and
reconstructive self-definition.

This dilemma was one of the harassing proportions of the
trial. Early on arose the question of Adam's identity. At first it
was generally assumed that he was Guianese (a native of
Albuoystown) but then the prisoner claimed he had come to
Albuoystown as a child and his mother was a Mosquito native
of Columbia, river Magdalena.

"Mosquito, mosquito," the judge thought giving his cheek
a gentle slap. "Why that's in Muisca, Columbia." He looked at
the prisoner with greater interest than ever. Racked his brains.
"Yes. I remember. El Dorado. Some historians claim *there*
(Mosquito or Muisca) was the site of Manoa (Alias El Dorado,
or gilded man)." He glanced through the window of the
aeroplane towards the mirror of the sun that flashed in his eyes
like gold. Others subscribed to different locations.

    The Empyre of *Guiana* is directly east from *Peru* to-
wards the sea, and lieth vnder the Equinoctial line, and it
hath more abundance of Golde than any part of *Peru,* and
as many or more great Cities than euer *Peru* had when it
flourished most; it is gouerned by the same lawes and the
Emperour and people observe the same religion, and the
same forme and pollicies in gouernment as was vsed in
Peru, not differing in any part: and as I have been assured
by such of the Spanyardes as haue seen *Manoa* the emperiall

Citie of *Guiana,* which the Spanyardes call *El Dorado,* that for the greatnes, for the riches, and for the excellent Seate; it farre exceedeth any of the world, at least such of the world as is knowen to the Spanish nation: it is founded vpon a lake of salt water of 200 leagues long like vnto *mare caspiu.*

"Beautiful mathematics," the judge mused, turning once again to the prisoner of memory, limbo bar. "For my part this poor devil Adam is no gilded man. And furthermore where is the true seat of El Dorado? If it is so fractured as to lie neither north nor south, east nor west, the Mosquito claim of Adam may constitute a splinter, splinter of authority." The judge scribbled on his pad away from the eyes of jurymen and officials – "It is the most remarkable obsession any prisoner has advanced in my time. *That the court which now tries him stands under the jurisdiction of another, far wiser, far greater.* He belongs, he says, to the gilded man, prince of the gilded housecoat. Poor devil, he's mad. There's no gold on him, he's black. A filthy welder, that's his trade. Why, in heaven's name, do I have to listen to his claim as though I am destined, in some extraordinary way, to fly there at the crack of doom, OH MY?"

There was an expression that Adam used at this moment which electrified the courtroom – "I sought to *unmake* myself to *make* something I had lost before I was born. The land that is nowhere. Manoa."

"Why then?" cried the judge, frustrated now and angry, "did you burn the factory down ?" He stared at Adam as at something or someone preposterously naïve: on one hand claiming the protection of a higher court in South America that had never existed – or if it had had long since been fractured and broken into a million parts like mosquitoes or wasps, Eumenides of the Amazon. (It was an unjust pun, the judge knew – Mosquito and mosquitoes, but he felt a stifling exasperation and annoyance which filled him with the desire to slap someone or something in the buzzing courtroom).

Perhaps – he restrained himself – the man was a communist/psychic agent born in Columbia (one of the legendary cradles of El Dorado) who had sleepwalked into Albuoystown and found it easy therefore to talk of a higher constitution, higher law, etc. and play at the same time the deadly game of the privileged saboteur. Throw dust in everybody's eyes as saint and devil.

The judge gave the sketch-pad before him a vicious stab. The voices of a parrot (labour-saving device) rang out like an orderly – "Order in the court please. Order in the court." The room grew silent, insulated like an aeroplane, and everyone now occupied two dimensions – technological roar without, caged psyche within: prisoner at the bar. The light from a mirror in the hands of a small boy at the back of the courtroom shone straight upon Adam, making him weep, not tears but dust which poured from his eyes. Poor dusty saint. Poor golden atomized devil. Communist paradise indeed. Manoa.

The small boy hid the mirror in his side as if having supplied the cue the prisoner (his father) needed, he wanted it to look accidental, not intentional.

Adam looked up (wretched sleepwalking welder, black El Dorado – the judge gave him a stab) "It was an accident," he said lamely as if he had forgotten his earlier plea about unmaking/making himself. And yet the self-same riddle masked his lips. "I lost my head," he said. "That's why I burnt bed and board. I challenge the constitution of this court. Too one-sided I say. How can it have *personal* authority over me when it cannot *feel*…?" He clutched the air as if it were a basket of lost features.

"My client is unwell," defending counsel said, "when he says *personal* he really means *impersonal*, my lord…"

"Vested in the person," cried Adam, "I mean *person*, person. No real authority in the person. This court – apart from the blasted witnesses who don't give a damn anyway – is not mine,

does not feel my existence at all. Doomed basket, I tell you...
the air I breathe... doomed... doomed..."

The judge adjusted the ventilator in the aeroplane. The
padded but curiously echoing silence oppressed him...
doomed... doomed ... doomed,... "Feel his existence," the judge
wrote on his pad away from the eyes of parrot or orderly.
"That's a new one. Never heard it before. Yes, he's a communist agent. No question of that. Raises an interesting question.
Is communism a basket of negatives – neither dust nor gold
but synthetic emotion? Does it, in fact, thrive on

   (a) the loss of spirituality from which it draws a kind of
      absent sanction, a kind of higher abstract appeal like a
      kingdom of sleepwalkers ?

   (b) the dialectic of materialism from which it draws a kind
      of plaster abstract martyrdom, a rejection of profit akin to
      idolatry or tyranny like a surplus of God prefabricated,
      preordained...?"

"My client is obviously a very sick man," defending counsel
said. "The sick man of the world. Brainwashed by ten-year
plan or ten-year accident (premium and policy) like a king of
insurance... Insurance for life... Insurance for death... All
contingencies."

"Is insurance and the communist plan then," said the judge
"emotive baskets of vacant proprietorship – life (earth), death
(heaven) – exploiting the collective subconscious to institu-
tionalize a victim – beneficiary in the name of ideal social *state*
or capital *self-interest*?"

He recalled the spectre of the mirror (small boy at the back
of the courtroom) – Adam's tears which were not tears but
which had been conscripted into an emotive synthesis of dust
or gold.

It was here for the first time, in fact, that he began indeed
to question his own synthetic authority and to wonder how
much truth lay in Adam's claim for a higher courtroom of
original feeling rather than quasi-feeling, a court which could

sift the entrenched reality of world-historical ruling intransigence, world-historical error, self-sufficient historical model, self-sufficient historical myth: a court which could rattle a world-historical chain compounded of dead men's bones illuminating and binding (like a lightning equation of serial reality and unreality) the very witnesses of the accused – his most intimate tragedies, fountainhead of tears – to a blighted iconography…

The judge stabbed the prisoner at the bar drawn on his pad. Communist agent. NO. Insurance agent. NO. But also YES. YES. Borderline alien person standing upon NO/YES whereby the quasi-liberal prosecution would feed on the sovereign sickness of an age (sovereign frustration NO to which assent nevertheless YES would unwittingly or wittingly be given in the name of collective idealism, sovereign fear NO to which assent nevertheless YES would unwittingly or wittingly be given in the name of collective security) and would fashion thereby its case in neo-Platonic terms, world-historical error, world-historical frame-up, world-historical imposition, world-historical racialism, the highest brute rationalization in the name of ideal self-sufficiency. And he – the judge – would be persuaded to sum up in a manner consistent with that uncanny mathematic of self-deception…

As such he and the officials of the court would confess – without apparently being aware of it – to their ruined personality and bow all unconscious it seemed to the prisoner at the bar as their straitjacket and sovereign, burden and collective witness. It was this question – not unfettered like to like – El Dorado to Plato – but browbeaten conformity – lack of feeling, quasi-feeling – entrenched in the brooding storm of psyche and nature; man and technology, which had flared in the judge as he boarded his plane bound for OH MY. So that *now* – once again – he was involved in a browbeaten synthesis but this time beyond all authoritarian emotional fortress –

beyond and beneath all crucifixions of the robot – into the lightning omen and revelation of true Christ as an organ of capacity for all men, dying Man. . . .

"OH CHRIST," said the judge scribbling on his pad. "OH MAGDALENE." It was the first time in forty years he tried to pray – aeroplane or courtroom.

The courtroom hummed like a bee. The defence counsel had summoned a new witness, Dr. Wall. "Alias Wall," scribbled the judge half-mockingly, half-seriously. "Assault on the fortress. Is this Christ's answer…?" He visualized parrot or orderly leaning over his shoulder through a breach in the plane to command the bee to sing until it roared in his ears ten million times louder like a gale through the upholstery of space. It was as if an old evolutionary *motif* in the hive of Manoa, reduced to clockwork numbers, woke now to a deeper functional tone of life and croaked like an oracle: parrot or raven. Two parrots, in fact, symbolic heralds of Manoa had perched on his shoulders like the ravens of Odin. "Christ-parrot, Christ-raven," wrote the judge on his pad. "Revelation's orderly."

"Breach in the wall," they screamed with a single vote. "Breach."

The judge looked out cautiously from behind his papers which shook now in his hands like the first human tremor of that gale, first questioning tremor forty years ago in the browbeaten clock of the parrot: increasing with the years, imperceptibly perhaps, but soon to blow beyond all measure – whirling his pages (the judge's poor likenesses of the judged) until they streamed in the wind like the confessional feathers of El Dorado married to death, marriage of serial ghosts; was it orderly raven or disorderly parrot the judge drew, caricature or archangel, gigantic wings banking on Omai?

It was this infinite organ of vacancy – net of likeness and unlikeness – within and without – that freed him (the judge) as it hammered him, that nailed him (the judged) as it trans-

71

lated him *through* and *beyond* sounding board or cross… aeroplane…

"Before I call Dr. Wall," said defence counsel, "I want to make my position as clear as I possibly can. My plea is based not on the behaviour of my client, as such, but on *feeling* tones and *unfeeling* relations beneath the gloss of behaviour, dead beak and claw which reinforce our irrational inclinations or disinclinations to condemn or release this man. In short I am concerned with the peculiar character of my client – his evolution, as it were, from nothing into a source of revelation."

There was a renewed buzz in the courtroom which quickly subsided now under the sudden glare of the judge like arclight or mirror in an operating theatre curving across the nightdress of the sky on to the brow of the sun. "Omen," the judge said to the parrot on one shoulder and the raven on the other. It wasn't a bad sketch, he thought, adding a line here and there to his novel history.

"Omen and revelation," cried defence counsel, "that's my plea, high judge, within world-historical idealistic straitjacket which my client dreads as much as he fears being edged out by this court – edged out of straitjacket on to the cross like another ornamental conceit, striped cat of god. Out of the museum into the coffin. That's why my client suspects everything, judge, parrot and raven, as ideological and mythological and technological furniture which takes offensive or defensive measures to preserve and extend its gloss on humanity…"

"I would be grateful if you would proceed to the matter of your new witness Dr. Wall – Alias Wall." There was suppressed laughter in the court – equation of comedy. "Is it sacred or black comedy?" asked the judge of striped cat, parrot and raven drawn on his pad.

"The witness Dr. Wall performed a caesarian operation on the wife of my client who, as you know, is the mother of the small boy Victor at the back of the courtroom (perched on rail or knob) with the mirror of subsistence planted in his side. Victor lived after the operation, mirror and all (Dr. Wall's sculpture) like a freak whose precocity began to alarm everyone (it seemed so out of place) though everyone wished to exploit it naturally to their hearts' contempt.

His mother died. Her death nearly killed Adam who began to feed upon a curious obsession – welder's obsession as Dr. Wall will tell you – about gnawing through ideological and technological fortresses. Something absurd and freakish as his conception of son and heir – death-dealing, life-giving accumulative appetite – without rhyme or reason.

And he came to feel that the nature of society or industry was like that. There were the lucky ones who feared and loathed the unlucky have-nots though they refused to admit it because, in effect, they (the haves) saw their accumulative fortunes as fundamentally arbitrary and ornamental which they needed to collectivize into a god of worth. There were the unlucky have-nots who hated and idolized the lucky haves though they refused to admit it because, in effect, they (the have-nots) saw their condition as fundamentally sinful and ugly which they needed to justify within a scapegoat – waxworks of the baboon.

Either way it was fundamentally an ornamentation of waste, a fixation of greed they enshrined so that, in fact, when they spoke of harmony and peace invariably they meant war (bloody wasteful war) and when they spoke of war invariably they meant a kind of insane hero-worship or anti-hero-worship, depending on the fashions of war and peace at the moment.

In fact my client was wrapped in an ornamental or technological cocoon, apotheosis of security fashioned out of assets of hostility he fantasied in nature in a manner, I plead, not unlike a certain view put brilliantly by Charles Darwin in *The Descent of Man* – (I quote) –

'The extraordinary size of the horns, and their widely

73

different structure in closely allied forms, indicate that they have been formed for some important purpose: but their excessive variability in the males of the same species leads to the inference that this purpose cannot be of a definite nature. The horns do not show marks of friction, as if used for ordinary work. Some authors suppose that as the males wander much more than the females, they require horns as a defense against their enemies; but in many cases the horns do not seem well adapted for defense, as they are not sharp. The most obvious conjecture is that they are used by the males for fighting together; but they have never been observed to fight, not could Mr. Bates, after a careful examination of numerous species, find any sufficient evidence in their mutilated or broken condition of their having been thus used… The conclusion which best agrees with the fact of the horns having been so immensely yet not so fixedly developed – as shown by their extreme variability in the same species and by their extreme diversity in closely allied species – is that they have been acquired as ornaments. This view will at first appear extremely improbable; but we shall hereafter find with many animals, standing much higher in the scale, namely fishes, amphibians, reptiles and birds, that various kinds of crests, knobs and horns have been developed apparently for this sole purpose.'

I hasten to add, high judge, that other researchers in this field disagree with Darwin and regard the horns of the beetle as articles of combat though some have been led to confess – as in respect of the stag beetles of England and the United States – that the method of fighting remains baffling and obscure…"

"Objection. Objection." Prosecuting counsel rose to his feet.

"Proceed with the nature of your objection," said the judge.

"My lord," said the prosecuting counsel, "the man on trial is a welder, a porknocker, a very ordinary though skilled Columbian/Guianese/Albuoystonian/El Doradonne/ Alias upon Alias *ignorant* labouring man. I think the line of inquiry adopted by defence counsel is completely irrelevant… He has put words already into his client's mouth…"

The judge polished off the horn he had been drawing on his pad. "Irrelevant, yes," he said, "but therein lies its curious aptness in this trial. It is the nature of irrelevance and the distinction one may draw between *ornament* and *amen of grace* that defence counsel wishes to establish on behalf of his client. As such the very absurdity of his line of inquiry – " the judge made rapid sketches on his pad looking through the window of his aeroplane – thirty-five thousand feet up – at projected shadow of the sky and projected brilliance of the sun – "carries within it a kind of fortuitous housecoat or barracks, instinctive lighthouse, like and unlike the gloom of his client.

In this respect defence counsel is setting the scene, the wall, the fortress, the factory, paradise (if you like), raven, parrot, mirror, knob, horn, etc., etc. which, we all know, has been breached time and time again but which we are still unable to scale – from above or beneath – since we don't know, in fact, whether we are trapped equally on the outside, as the inside, by subconscious or unconscious glories which we deny but nevertheless appeal to like sleepwalkers – or by the sheer callous bounty of nature which we stiffen into a barren shield or shell or scapegoat. If, in fact, defence counsel, even now, in this apparently late age of the aeroplane (within an hour or two of OH MY) can begin to sift the distinction between omen of grace (terrestrial/transcendental lighthouse, subsistence of memory) and tenant of fantasy, it may be possible to reverse the sentence of the court…"

"Thank you, high judge," said defence counsel. "And now my first submission is Item A on behalf of Alias Wall (which I have labelled Fetish) and it is of hypnotic relevance (or irrelevance) to this trial. As Dr. Wall – through his other parties will testify – it was obtained from my client under hypnosis. It is, in fact, a peculiar kind of poem notable for its obsession with ornament within which runs, I plead, an ominous state or clarity germane to the style of these proceedings. There are many, of course, who will, until doomsday, refuse to see what I mean. And this is not surprising since one is involved at a certain level in an abnormal irrelevancy as Fetish indicates. I would like to draw your attention, judge, to images like *pursuit of stains like flowers* or *gnome of the sky roots in sawdust and red shavings* or *old sunlight and brandished veins,* etc., etc. All these reappearing finally as *dry sticks and dusty leaves* (which) *paint the individual storm.*

High judge I make no claim for this poem as good or bad except to point to its genuine peculiarity: it possesses an ornamentation of features, a fixation with excess which is related, as I said before, to a state of besieged or besieging soul. Apart from this omen it may be regarded as a conceit about death –

skeleton clothed and unclothed

who thrusts a bone into the blinding mirror –

the conceit of death which – if we shed the conflicting graces of the soul – is all that would remain to mankind to gloss a meaningless existence."

The judge leaned forward and accepted Item A (Fetish) concealing, as best he could, the gale of embarrassment that sought to rip the pages from his fingers – intuition of the skeleton of OH MY. He felt the reality of that gale within his blood, a kind of stoical cloak he and his peers had long cultivated. He was only too well aware that he had himself overruled the objection of prosecuting counsel to defence counsel's tactics. But now had come an unpalatable moment of truth. He had so far been fascinated by defence counsel's unlicensed gifts, cultivated brainstorm, proletarian sympathies, the words he had put into his client's mouth. But while these might be permissible an hour or two from OH MY – coming from one of his own profession – he was still unprepared to face the fact that the untutored prisoner himself could speak out of the subconscious, on his own behalf, like a dead portrait consistent with its own voice of nothingness in order to blast the pretensions of all who made a living by dubbing those, whose cause they espoused, with their own noises of emancipation or tyranny.

If he (the untutored prisoner speaking now through Fetish) had to be dubbed and gagged like the picture of a slave on a wall, better to be truly obscure when he croaked through his welded lips than to wear a false light or coherent function of robot on his brow, dawn of a uniform callous.

The judge sighed. He knew before he glanced at Fetish he would dislike it – would label it pretentious of sovereign prisoner and witness he had long silenced in his dreams. And yet it was not too late anyway to begin to do so – open dislikes, open labels, even intellectual dishonesties on his part were better than no feeling or reaction at all for centuries an hour or two from OH MY.

FETISH

Drowned darkness
is the pursuit of stains like flowers:
the wide and solitary gnome of the sky roots

in sawdust and red shavings
but earthbound living cheeks
are too solemn to be punctured
by splinters of the wind driving from off
unseen river's
ribbed watermarks and blue clouds

until translucent curiosity contrives upon the mood of still
death
a frail entrance and exit for the spirit:
a channel into the furious sky:
wings borne beyond the edge of artificial

raindrops falling from the shop roof of space
on skeleton clothed and unclothed
who thrusts a bone into the blinding mirror
of bright and fantastic river

in pitiful assumption of vision
beside the immense glare of water and sky

or only more loveless vacant eye
against pale subdued bar of a disquieting finger
pointing
to old sunlight and brandished veins spectacular
patched unvariations of colour
otherwise gaiety of the unnatural relief of gloom
under domination of the spiritual landscape
and ambush of perennial ghost. Whose heaven
is imagination of freedom
the inaccessible moment of strange release
bordered with white emphasis and torn into shadows of
reproach
playful beyond tiny figures doomcovered and naked
like angels.
Human flesh grows wrinkled
or luminous
discarding a remote and angelic fury
growing nostalgic perhaps for the night
and odour of the living release from fire

dreamless perhaps
in touch of daylight upon hard hidden colour

vain perhaps
with treasure of the moonthatched hair fallen into
disrepute

hungry perhaps
like empty mouth dark with carven pain on a huge
    forehead

And the dreamless borderless sky changes to watch
the way the fever dies on intent particles of light:

calm perhaps
like unruffled cloud vastly contingent upon gloom:

dry sticks and dusty leaves paint the individual storm.

As the judge read the lines, parrot and raven croaked the words
across the courtroom. Prosecuting counsel rose to his feet.
"Quite absurd. Quite absurd." Judge nodded as if he partly
agreed with prosecuting counsel, partly dreamt of his courtroom within a projected screen of night and day upon Omai:
enormous interwoven vessels of the law from the beginning
of time, myths of the law, trial of the soul, creation myths,
invention myths, wars of the roses, Odin of the ravens,
Quetzalcoatl, El Dorado of the parrots, Fauna and Flora of
history... As a great general in retirement dreams of conquest
so judge – in his flight to OH MY – dreamt of the fetish of the
conquered...

"It's a kind of rubbish heap of images," prosecuting counsel
cried, "compounded of bunk – the blasted bunk of civilizations." The judge scribbled *blasted bunk* on his pad.

"The kind of mirage," prosecuting counsel continued,
"one brings back from dreams or from drugs (at least so I'm
told by the Dr. Walls of this world). Reminds me personally
of certain primitive borderline areas in the Tropics. Bunk of all
kinds. The bones of dead sawmills, mattresses, housecoats,
shattered sculpture, carcases of the motor car, mastheads and
stranded skins or sails on the riverfront. It's infectious – this
Fetish lunacy. Though some make a business of it since it's

hard at times to distinguish the living from the dead aboriginal antique of memory. All that exotic pseudo-historical rubbish. I know the atmosphere so well – have been steeped in it since I was a boy (my father was a travelling magistrate and district commissioner). I know the sort of splintered world – neither capitalist nor communist. The museum of man. Left Bank manifesto stuff. The French have a flair for it – a nose for both the genuine buried article and the fake dressed in moonthatched hair, neo-Gauguin. I never had any illusions, I assure defence counsel, about the enormous callous of insensibility that seeks to invest in everything, which has gone before, and to mimic the courage of desolation. Overplayed guitar in the middle of nowhere. It's so uninspiring, so weak in this day and age…"

"Weak, yes," said defence counsel. "But there's the true confessional spirit of the present, and restorative medium of the future. Fetish is a poem about disintegration – you perceive the implicit foundation or lack of foundation very well – but you are unable to see you are being *assisted,* as it were, to break the callous you deplore: there lies the ominous dereliction – the unpretentious clarity of Fetish…"

"The rubbish of civilizations you mean. What a mess Fetish is…"

"Yes, indeed what a mess. But mess – rubbish – is invaluable. It is, in fact, a new experimental source of wealth. Everything depends on whether you are serious about it or cynical about it. If you're serious you won't just sweep it under the carpet and invest, after that, in a number of tidy self-indulgent rationalizations which ignore the light of the future. Fetish seeks to break this *tidiness* because, in fact, it's all part of a callous or callouses of conceit we plaster upon everything. You and I appear to agree about this. As Dr. Wall will tell you – and his interest in Fetish is less in the poem than in the borderline depressive state of Adam (buried, no doubt, as you rightly imply in left bank manifestos and museums of man, exotic rubbish heaps and reservations) – as

Dr. Wall will tell you, I repeat, what Adam is trying to salvage or uncover is a sacramental vacancy within the flotsam and jetsam of a collective experience that has oppressed him and continues to oppress him in the name of a puritanical humanity, whereas it may well be the fuel of a compassionate divinity…"

"Dr. Wall is an idiot."

"Depends on your point of view. Clown or saviour – like the cross. May I continue with my plea?"

The judge nodded, partly assenting, partly dreaming of his courtroom within a projected screen of day and night… novel or novel history.

"With the death of his wife, Adam was filled with the most violent suicidal complex. Part reaction to the harshness he had himself cultivated for years (within his welder's mask, *persona* of the factory): suffering and pain had become commonplace to him in the slave market of technology. When his wife died he became easy meat for demagogue or fixation, curse or blessing, deity or child which stood now on the housetops of Albuoystown and flashed its mirror of the merry-go-round into his eyes – *Why do the well get steadily weller* (sic), *the rich steadily richer, the poor poorer, the sick sicker…? Why couldn't your wife live, Adam, on the merry-go-round, why couldn't she be given an injection, painless* (hip) *birth and all that…?*

When Dr. Wall came into the picture it was too late to stop Adam from burning the factory down. It was sheer fun – desensitized (sick) self-portrait – black comedy, sacred irony…"

"I question your line of argument. This is 1929. Forty years hence things may be different. But now we are a poor country in an obscure still untapped continent. Our hospitals are poorly equipped, Mosquito or El Dorado. It's nobody's fault that Adam's wife died. Furthermore what, in God's name, has Fetish to do with this?"

"Fetish," said defence counsel patiently, "contains the seeds of alternatives since it's always, as you say, nobody's fault…"

"Seedy alternatives you mean," said prosecuting counsel.

"Seeds of alternatives since in salvaging a borderline reality from the subconscious and unconscious it refuses to enthrone indifference upon the swings of history but seeks very inadequately, I agree, *seeks nevertheless,* a residual distinction within a flamboyance of models…"

"But what good can possibly come of it…?"

"It seeks to lay bare the dereliction of the primitive fetish as in uneasy frail collaboration with Christian omen or sacrament, light or vision, a quality of frailty that distinguishes a true involvement with flesh-and-blood within the brute masks of history…"

"My lord," said prosecuting counsel, "I would like to express my profound uneasiness with defence counsel's line of country. And furthermore to voice my outrage that his client's Fetish is – according to his own confession – the work of hypnosis. Brute mask indeed. I think the precedent is an extremely dangerous one…" The judge nodded. "What have you to say to this, defence counsel?" he asked, sniffing the feather of parrot or raven as if he smelt sulphur.

"High judge," said defence counsel, "I am only too well aware of the territory I tread. There are sulphur mines on Omai as well as gold and silver. I know that hypnosis can incur an extreme erasure of memory or extreme solidification of memory. Neither casualty – as Dr. Wall will testify – is a feature of my client's hypnosis. Dr. Wall has gone to great pains to use hypnosis as a therapeutic dimension wherein my client can find borderline territory – insulation/annihilation frontiers. As such memory becomes a delicate screen to sift a balance a natures, which – if one were subject to them in an extreme form – would mean psychosis, that is impossible self-rejection (total loss) or impossible self-fulfilment (total gain).

It is true, my lord, such a balance (loss/gain) – such an organ of digestion (through a measure of insulation from our task by which we prepare ourselves for our task, through a measure of

annihilation in our task through which we subjectively im-
merse ourselves in our task) is an ideal – some believe – of a
divine ecology, paradise or Eden: or the goal – as others think
– of an imperfect world-fortress whose excesses and violations
we seek to compensate within a continuous striving for balance, compensation-ritual (likeness/ unlikeness, loss/gain) we
can only *strive* to attain.

It is in this therapeutic, endless, preparatory, working
dimension that my client became the patient of Dr. Wall and
he will remain so – with the consent and knowledge of this
court – until sentence is passed. By sentence, high judge, I am
concerned with your decision on omen and revelation."

Prosecuting counsel interrupted – "Defence counsel," he
said scathingly, "is intent on reducing this court to a metaphysical jungle or a historical jungle. Omen and revelation…
what does he mean?"

"I mean, my lord, that the ornament of nature, the bounty of
nature, property, etc. (and remember my client stands accused
of sabotage) if viewed as excess baggage from cradle to grave,
acquired and shed according to fortune (long or short, good or
bad) – if viewed in this way – is the blatant conceit of death.
Fortuitous and meaningless really. If viewed, on the other hand,
as an omen of grace, it possesses, within every cloak of darkness,
a frail light – (a sacramental feeling for reconciling the divided
heritage of man) – which shines *through* every burden of acqui-
sition as that burden inevitably disperses itself within an imperfect material constitution. It is this dispersal or disintegration
through which the sacramental union or balance shines to
transform the quality of our participation in the quantitative
joys and woes of all mankind…

That *light* of *omen* is, I plead, high judge, the mystery of life-
in-death, death-in-life; it brings grace, I believe, where nothing else appears to inform unfeeling fortune.

And also it brings alternatives within history – frail, subtle
but lasting alternatives – in that the light from son to father,

Victor to Adam, new to old, generation to generation, stranger to stranger, judged to judge, etc., etc., can offer the mathematics of freedom, the map of adventure, idealism, morality provided we do not succumb to euphoria at any stage and in that fixation block our goal of balance in the future by identifying a transient model with a vacancy of origins (by arbitrarily and impossibly – so to speak – filling the void)…"

"Are you telling this court," said the judge nodding against the upholstery of the aircraft, "and by the way I take it you will bring a considerable body of evidence to support your novel history – are you telling us that the light of grace, omen, what-have-you, this sacramental union of life and death (if I understand you aright), pain and joy, opposite existences – exists fundamentally upon a curvature of ruined personality within which we subsist by degrees, degrees of insulation when we appear blessed by arbitrary fortune, degrees of annihilation when we appear cursed by fortune ?"

"Precisely, my lord. And further that there would be no prospect of balance if it were not for this omen of grace which is accompanied not only by fortune, but by fortune's ghosts, in that fortune, because of her waywardness, can animate intuitions of splendour or intuitions of crisis and downfall – can, as it were, set up its own spectres *before* and *after* an event and thus from its inferior ground of rank superstition come into uneasy collaboration with *spirit,* as fetish collaborates with *omen.*"

"I take it, defence counsel, you will now seek to identify – on behalf of your client – some of these spectres of history…"

"I shall do my best, high judge, my poor best. For I am nobody's everybody and everybody's nobody…"

(LAUGHTER IN THE COURT TINCTURED BY UNEASINESS AND EMBARRASSMENT.)

"He's our clown of clowns, poor fool, idiot," said prosecuting counsel.

"Everybody's clown, nobody's fool," scribbled the judge, his mind wandering a little.

7

Judge nodded in the aeroplane, half-asleep, half-awake. He shuffled the sketches on his lap like a pack of cards – the curious sketches and records he had made forty years ago as he attended to the conventional noises of the court: secret sketches to record the other *silent* voices he felt beneath everyone and everything: *mute* sensations (Cezanne would have called them "ma petite sensation") that returned to address him as if he, himself, were on trial, and what had *not* been said then was endeavouring to be heard now.

Throughout the years, in fact, and even now on the aeroplane he still found himself elaborating on those sketches – adding a line here or a dot there – and rearranging it all too in the mind of dreams minute by minute with pencils of light, pencils of the imagination.

Those pencils *spoke* by illumining the curious disintegration of the past and invoking through the granular sensation of images – the dust of memory, the rubbish heap of landscape – a sequence of words allied not simply to pictures but to the very brokenness of all fabric inherent in vision. *Language for him, therefore, was a vision of consciousness as if what one dreams of in the past is there with a new reality never so expressive before because nothing stands now to block the essential intercourse of its parts, however mute, however irrelevant.*

There was the sketch, for example, of the raven and the parrot on his shoulders. The judge smiled at the self-portrait compounded of himself and the solemn orderlies of the court. Earthy-looking mathematical/mythical creatures, crude draughtsmanship, strong body, thick lines of man and bird which seemed obscurely as well as clearly related to some ancient half-whole, half-broken community of illusion or adventure. Whether the obscurity lay in the unfulfilled adventure, the clarity in the blocks of illusion, was something he still had to discover.

There was the mirror in Victor's side, too, flashing on Adam's brow from the back of the courtroom. (This had been his private poetic interpretation of a beam of light darting by accident or intention from the small boy at the back of the room, as though that small boy could be, in fact, the author of himself *now* – judge/judged – psychic/technological storehouse).

There was the arc-light, too, he had drawn on his own brow when he glared at the courtroom for silence when defence counsel spoke of the operating theatre where Adam's wife died: a terrifying climax: the lines were smudged: could they equally be welder's brow, judge's eye, caesarian globe?

The judge sighed. As modern – he consoled himself – as the latest invention, and yet (glancing at the sky) reminiscent of the cosmology of myth, housecoat of stars, etc.

There was the sketch of Darwin's horn, half-ornamental, half-obscure. The music of the spheres. Symphony of evolution.

There was the sketch of Dr. Wall. The judge smiled again: the air of a man who wept. Wiped his eyes in which a speck of the aeroplane had settled. Out of the dust of the past, floating across the years, he visualized someone, in fact, who had never been there at all, never been summoned at all. His name had been mentioned several times during the trial but for some reason the judge could not recall he had not actually appeared. Yet – beyond a shadow of doubt – his presence, through the gestures of defence counsel, was so real it appeared at times to blend into the very furniture of the room. To blend into the sketches the judge made: he had drawn a hole in the court-room – in the aeroplane – poor Wall – within which a series of magical, comical pictures, fetishes, investitures, therapies stood and vanished. This enigma was the essence of the witness Alias Wall whose eloquence sprang from gesture like a charade of conscience: whose voice sprang from nothingness like an archetype of silence, compounded of Alias Tin, Alias Copper, Alias Picket, *circumambulatio* of courtroom, school, factory, door, exit, entrance: theatre and cosmos, shadow and sun, ruined personality within whose rubbish shone nevertheless an illumination of function that could divest itself of the over-burden of appetite by subsistence of memory (the frail but measureless participation of Christ).

"Time," said defence counsel, "is the spectre of humanity. Look – there – my lord – your own sketch – breach in the wall. The cross of OH MY: universal porknocker – ruined labour, ruined capital, ruined captor, ruined captive, ruined adven-turer. Far in advance of its time even now – this cross, breach, call it what you will – as it recedes in the wall into a derelict basket of thrones and confessions – *one* frail thread – call it unity, call it love – within and beyond all."

The judge shuffled his sketches like a pack of cards. There was one (in fact several) he realized he had overlooked. A calendar of days of the years, for example, crossed for holidays, saints' days, courtroom days, etc. One such cross he had inscribed *Day of the Prisoner, black welder; Almanac of El Dorado, Vicar of Mosquito, factory of the gilded man at the heart of a slum; courtroom of the soul.*

Had time – the judge weighed the spectre in his mind – had the years since 1929 when the trial began, hung heavy and secure, padlock and prison; or light and insecure, feather of Manoa, stigmata of the void?

"Why," the judge groaned, glancing at his watch, coiled instinct, spring of alarm (*doomed… doomed… unless…*) "why," he repeated, "were he and all men so obsessed by the clock – whether black welder or white scrivener, clerk of court or registrar of births – prisoners of time, in time, sentenced, paroled ?

Contrary to what anyone might think," the judge continued to address his pad, "it wasn't a rhetorical question. It was a question about obsession with security, with material security, with force, violence, material origin, masks of adventure, masks of history. For the claim of OMAI/OH MY – factory of Albuoystown, gold, oil, silver or base metal, soil of industry – lay within the vision of time either as the vessel of humanity (part and parcel of the inalienable universal scrap-heap of time, taste of universality, ground of spirituality, bitter-sweet, like/unlike, black/white) or as a gaol, the Midas self-destructive touch, the callous of technological achievement, indigestible baggage from cradle to grave.

There were those who cried that the wealth of man belonged to an aboriginal calendar (black man's sacred burden): others who shouted it had been visibly exploited and vested in a technological profanity (white man's civilization). Either way it became a prisonhouse at war with itself in the name of security/insecurity in which the ghost of time appeared to languish or prosper within a vicarious humanity, archaic banner and conception or rich and sophisticated label."

Dr. Wall's testimony – the judge half-smiled, half-sighed, looking up from his writing-pad – embodied this supreme contradiction, conviction of a terrifying gaol or fortress whose *silence* was fraught with the deepest most painful eloquence of stunned reflexes on behalf of *freedom*. As defence counsel's chief witness he (Alias Wall) remained in hiding, poetic license, sacred irony: subject therefore to the true voice of feeling, body of patience, vessel of time. Subject not only to chained limbs but chained tongues, vice-like grip. It was this on behalf of which he witnessed. Vice or soul within the clock that struck – in spite of itself – the half-caste hours (freedom and unfreedom, art and science, duty and compassion, sub-sistence and greed, quantitative synthesis, browbeaten time, qualitative light, redemptive time, OH MY).

In this way the very gestures of defence counsel in conform-ing to a picture were signals of the stigmata of the void pressing upon time to enlarge the minute links between fetish of the clock and every bone of enterprise, carcass of the motorcar and every ornament of grace, rubbish heap of the past and every revelation of the future, black welder, red Prometheus, masks of fire and blood.

A fantastic kind of pentecostal masculine/feminine brood-ing light, charisma of motherhood (MAGDALENE), flux of fatherhood (CHRIST), voices within voices, lamentations and blues, Negro/Jewish/Toltec/American/African/European, etc., etc. *The judge made rapid gnomic scribbles as he addressed his pad*. Dr. Wall's theory of the chasm of the womb, submerged bridge, hypnosis of relief, was in advance of its time in the primitive hospital of Albuoystown and it aroused the deepest misgivings in his colleagues who saw him as a Schweitzer of the parasite of the soul. Sacred comedy. Reverence for life and death, disease as a therapeutic omen of identity.

"Time," said defence counsel, "as Dr. Wall knows… knows… is the spectre… spectre… of humanity…"

The judge shuffled his pack: Jack of trades, scavenger and sovereign of spirits, housecoat of stars, breadwinner of suns. He was suddenly stricken by a sense of "emptiness" as though the characters he attacked or defended, also attacked him *in his own monolithic name,* defended him blindly as compassionate alien within mandala or fortress. They were as much his disabled creation as he theirs – all roles were interchangeable – judge, judged, victor, victim, Adam, etc., etc. as parts of a broken translation and legacy of history.

They and he constituted a spectral host advancing from a citadel or form to the same blinding citadel, misconception or form. And here, in fact, he saw the relevance of Dr. Wall's view of character. Character – in Wall's crumbling perspective – was like and unlike its own conscious formulations of activity. So engrossed in the gamble of time, it possessed a kind of blind clarity that became the paradoxical legacy of history, ironic security, feud and murder, through which agent upon agent was drawn, hanged, quartered, born, reborn, disfigured, trans-figured in a drama of community, spectre of community, lightning equation, self-besieged, self-besieger. So blindly engrossed (Wall's character was) it made war upon time itself, the spectre of time itself, as the ultimate enemy of reason which it sought to conscript as its material base.

The judge shuffled his cards with a sigh. He wanted, he knew, to write a kind of novel or novel history in which the spectre of time was the main character, and the art of narrative the obsessed ground/lighthouse of security/insecurity.

And as such – the judge shuffled the blank cards in his pack – there was room for endless participants, critic, friend, lover, enemy ascending OH MY, whose verdict would underwrite his book like a groundswell of fear or longing that time, obscure time, would bring all things to a close. Obscure time. The judge weighed each blank in his pack. Who would attack, who defend? Would they damn his work as meddling, absurd, Columbian, Mexican, El Doradonne?

Perhaps it would help, the judge decided, if he aired his basket a little in order to make the sieve of tradition clear. This obsession with time as comma and period, age and full-stop, was, in his view, something that sprang from a base idolatry, from a desire to conscript time itself into a material commod-ity. It was instructive to trace the weight of this conception through many cultures and civilizations that exposed both a material predilection for storing time as well as *angst* at the leakage of time. Take, for example, pre-Columbian Mexican character.

This, in fact, had a close bearing on the judge's novel in that his choice of forty years was a symbolic equivalent to the

Mexican cycle of fifty-two years. Also the judge's cards and sketches were a symbolic equivalent to the Mexican sheaf of time, series of time which bore a correspondence to one of spades, two of hearts, three of diamonds, four of clubs, five of spades, six of hearts, seven of diamonds, eight of clubs, etc. Again the judge's indeterminate sets and colours, parrot, raven, rose, etc. were a symbolic equivalent to the ancient Mexican calendar, rabbits, reeds, flints, houses.

There was, however, a profound distinction the judge wished to imply in his vision of time *vis-à-vis* the ancient Mexican obsession with a sheaf or game. The distinction was an important one. It could be stated in this way: the Mexicans – precisely because they wished to conscript time on a material base – were drawn every fifty-two years by their fear that time had to be manufactured afresh (the game needed to commence afresh) or it would slip from their grasp forever.

Thus they seized on a victim – on flesh-and-blood as their fortress or factory of time – and tore the living heart out as from a rabbit, stuffed rabbit. Then by firing this base they greeted the bank of the sun as a new dawn, newly-minted time.

The judge, on the other hand, precisely because he wished a qualitative illumination to emerge in his novel history rather than a quantitative bank of time, saw – beforehand – into the unique density and transparency of his victim (spectral character and dust) and refrained therefore from inflicting a senseless ordeal on what was in essence the ghost of the universe, serial participation in time, universal subsistence of memory, mature void, immaterial function, mature vacancy, non-idolatrous fixation.

He pulled a card from his pack. PROPHET had been written there. Yes – the judge sighed – he would be accused of being vatic. How could he begin to explain to the ignorant and impatient that *time,* year and day, was involved in his prophecies as a spectral function within which like/unlike – the ruined fortress of personality – could subsist *now* as *then* (today or a thousand years hence) as *blank* cheque of compassion rather than bankrupt materialism or passion? As a consciousness without content which nonetheless permitted all alien contents to exist: as stigmata of the void equivalent to the frailest felt cross of humanity, the wine of sacrifice, acute needle, perilous sensation, depths of healing, abyss of humility rather than overstimulation, uniform prejudice, callous throne, heights of the banal.

8

The judge glanced at the sky from the window of his aeroplane and shuffled his deck of cards. He could see far below him in the mist of the late afternoon what looked like the spirit of a town, settlement or harbour, whale of a ship lit from stem to stern sailing beneath the clouds across parrot's ocean or peacock's wave: flying-fish of El Dorado. It reminded him of his own phantasmagoric sketches, illuminated rainbow of night, the night Adam had set fire to the factory, grown berserk, run through Albuoystown to his own home where he burnt bed and board.

Victor had wandered off with a companion that evening for a game of marbles. Earlier (remember? the judge consulted his sketches) Victor had perched on the wall of the warehouse above the river: a whale of a steamer went by. Perched on the wall with his mirror and waited unsuccessfully for his father to appear at the door of the factory. "Do you remember?" the judge addressed the hidden *personae* in his pack, blurred masks or readers looking over his shoulder backwards from the future: flicked the pages of his book like an expert gambler with currencies of time – obverse and reverse. On one side *judge* on the other *judged*. On one side again *father* on the other *son*. On one side still again *ancient* on the other *modern*. There it was, he cried, *whale of a steamer* seen through Victor's eyes (Alias judge's eyes forty years later as the plane moved over the lost city of Manoa and great figures of cloud intervened within and upon sea or harbour, ocean or river of El Dorado). The judge reread the page of his novel written long before and stitched to the sketch of the warehouse wall, like currency of time, omen of posterity, genealogy of the robot.

It ran as follows;

"There was an old wall running around a disused warehouse – much higher than the fence of St. Saviour's Churchyard. This would afford him anew the angle and coincidence he needed – an hour or so before sunset – metamorphosis of metals.

It gave him (as he waited for his father to come) a view of the river, white, beaten gold at first, turning magnificently and slowly into scarlet lion, bronze child, cloud, sailing-vessel, fishing-craft, rocking tub under a feather. A whale of a steamer began to appear – doubledecker of sunset. Still no sign of his father.

Who knows (Victor dreamt) – he may have been transferred there, for a day or two, on that whale of a steamer. An expert welding job. Bauxite money. Aluminium. Fish to melt in his mouth. Overtime. Victor wondered whether one day he would own not only racehorses but bauxite plants in Demerara, aluminium processing factories in Canada. Atlantic ferry. Fleet of buses. Own it as if it were light as a feather. Gossamer scale. Petticoat made of butter. Bullet made of security. Self-ironical light, theatre of bread, sunset, porknocker's boudoir. *Still no sign of his father.*

Victor felt curiously alarmed. There had been talk for weeks now of a general strike which would involve the factory. *No sign of his father, stable of the underground.* It had come – yes – he felt it in his bones – the Strike…

It would mean (he cursed softly) once again tightening his belt. His allowance had been increased – bread and meat – overtime. But with a strike everything would go back to starvation level. He was torn – hatred and idolatry. Hatred of the factory. STRIKE, YES, WHY NOT? Idolatry of bread, idolatry of meat, idolatry of capital. STRIKE, NO, NOT NOW.

He could hear voices at the bottom of the chasm, then a single voice it seemed talking back and forth, talking to him, rubbing it in. Self-absorption. He had been caned that day in school for burning a hole in his exercise book. Heat of the sun. Blazing mirror. 'Daylight robbery,' schoolmaster and judge had said. 'Taxpayers' money.'

'Twelve strokes of the cat,' the voice in the chasm intoned. 'Man of brimstone. Sentenced by the court.' Victor felt accused, accursed, humiliated, embarrassed. Embarrassed and humiliated by nightmare robot he had been inclined to take for granted, unfurnished cane, unfeeling yoke (master and slave). As if the ironic counterpoint which had been a source of emancipation before, vacant millions, had begun to sear him to the bone. He remembered. ON THE HILL WHERE HE LAY FORTY YEARS LATER THE STRIKE BEGAN TO RETURN. SIX MONTHS OF STRIKE. BURNING OF FACTORY BY HIS FATHER OR FATHER'S MATE. SENTENCED TO THE CAT. SEVEN YEARS' HARD LABOUR.

Brimstone had been his father's mirror, father's shadow. Sat side by side on the same bench… factory. Close friends from far back, schooldays. Same name, same build. *Adam.* Some people were confused when sentence was passed – were they one and the same… shadow… mate… conscience?

Dubbed a mysteryman, cane-breaker at school… hard ass… workbench. Lost his hide, job. Lost his scholarship (Victor's imagination moved in concert now with the robot in his side – robot prisoner, robot millions)."

The judge stopped reading having come to the end of his page and drew instead the faceless outline of a gentle reader, fierce parrot, sardonic raven. Through the window of his aeroplane the lost city of Manoa had become like a pool in the clouds into which a stone, *lapis* of ambivalences, had fallen, and concentric rings representing frontiers of memory spread across the sea of the atmosphere. The passage he had consulted a moment ago of Victor on the warehouse wall, Victor on the hill of Omai recalling the mirror of childhood, recalling Adam or Adam's mate, possessed for him not a confusion of identity but a confession of density and transparency that the ripples on the surface of space – ripples of adventure could be seen as identical with *either*

    (a) a fortress of illusion buried in a preconception of history, in a rigidity of psyche; *or*

    (b) an omen of community in depth.

As (a) – in its capacity as self-generative illusion or fortress, base of fear it could drown or override all current of communication between man and man in a wave of bias. Drown and blast all like an unreflective swamp – uniform cause, uniform effect, uniform action, uniform reaction.

As (b) omen of depth, it became the dark mirror of judgement seat, plane of equations, qualitative telescope, fire and water, atom and pool, whose concentric horizons moved from an inner plumb-bob or event – an inner lighthouse whose store of energy reactivated horizons of conquest as subsistence of grace or memory: sanctification of dead/living space.

It was this conception of the sanctification of space that occupied the judge as fundamental to his novel history of the gilded man, the black welder of Albuoystown, the lost kingdom of Manoa. He had, in fact, prepared a sketch shown hereunder:

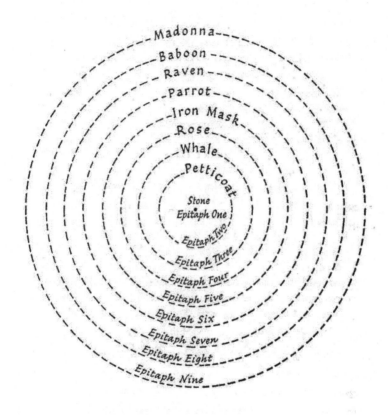

Madonna
Baboon
Raven
Parrot
Iron Mask
Rose
Whale
Petticoat

Stone
Epitaph One
Epitaph Two
Epitaph Three
Epitaph Four
Epitaph Five
Epitaph Six
Epitaph Seven
Epitaph Eight
Epitaph Nine

FACTORY OF THE GILDED MAN

1. Frontiers of conquest/death
2. Terrestrial/transcendental lighthouse

Amongst Victor's earliest memories *(ma petite sensation)* was the feel of stone – bruises on his knees. He could hardly have been more than three-and-a-half when, running into the street from the boarding-house where his father lived, he was suddenly aware of an approaching car: almost on top of him: shriek of brakes. It was a narrow shave: the car had stopped an inch from his brow where he had fallen on the ground unhurt save for a sharp cut on his knee from a stone in the roadway.

It was a minor bruise actually though with the car almost on top of him he felt he had been cut to rib and heart and that the stone itself *bled*. It was curious but in the hubbub of passersby and the outcry of the driver of the car, a nothingness enveloped him, like a muffled drum in the sun, a singing stone, something faint, voiceless *and yet he could hear it distinctly*. Something to do with the buried tongues of consciousness, African, Manoan ancestors, limbo dancers of Albuoystown, the masked dead of several continents and centuries who passed his door on holidays and holy days; a week before he had seen them, the very day, in fact, the Salvation Army stood at the corner and sang hymns and read a passage from the Bible. It was a peculiar series of identifications: painted stone, burning kneecap, limbo personality, Salvation Army. He remembered the woman dressed like a picture (she wore a sash of blood-red he dreamt) who in the interval between two hymns the small party sang, read a passage from the Bible:

> "And the devil said unto him, If
> thou be the Son of God, command
> this stone that it be made bread.
> And Jesus answered him, saying,
> It is written, That man shall
> not live by bread alone, but by
> every word of God."

Victor looked down at the stone there which, painted on the highway, had seemed to him, in an instant, evocative of something he could not describe – ancient as the role of saviour and subsistence, the role of hunter and hunted, tempter and tempted, voice of feeling... It was a dream from which, on opening his eyes (his father stood above him, having run into the street summoned by the crowd) the light of reflection from the windscreen on the car struck him on the brow as if it came from his own spear and side (rather than from the car's mirror) and in the urgency of that flash, he (the son) stored an equation of lightning, whereas he (the father) stored a mask of response that the child, after all, lying there so still *was dead* upon the frontiers of instinct.

Perhaps in truth he died then (one serial configuration or possibility in him) as he had died before at birth (another serial flash when his mother fell to little Caesar), as he was to die again and again, and the horizons of conquest were to be painted on stone or wood or cloth or glass or tin or copper or gold or feather or fish or marble...

A year later – after the near-fatal accident – Victor found the selfsame bleeding stone in the middle of the highway where it had been kicked out of the ground by the ironclad wheel of a cart. He was sure this was the one beneath which he lay – one picture of himself fallen there, paint or blood, drummerboy, choirboy of memory.

He picked it up: epitaph or stone which had bled for him not only then when his heart appeared to stop under the car but long ago on an operating-table beneath the arc-light of Dr. Wall, field-marshall, judge, hypnotist, gynaecologist. He "remembered" it now: limbo mother: limbo father: limbo judge: FORTY YEARS LATER ON OH MY: series of numb identifications, flashing wall-within-wall-within-wall... *circumambulatio* of sun and soul, equations of destiny, rowdy band of the elements. Only yesterday his father had given him an ominous tap and addressed him as "little Caesar" – the name, in fact, of one of the major performers of the limbo dance on Olympus or Albuoystown. Ascent to Omai. He felt the devil of power rise and choke him to strike back with a fist of stone. On his lips a frozen cry of injustice: how could the crystallization of pain be so fierce as to make him confront a cyclic monster within and linear beast without? Make him want to sculpt and create an animal of fear in his own and his father's name – blue-print or devil, welder or fortress, insurance policy, sabotage?

A feeling of unreality enveloped him – ironic and tormenting – since this was all (unreal as it was, spectral, fleeting) that partially redeemed him of sovereign technological psychic illusion. It stripped his fingers like a ghost of numb obsession: he unclasped the stone and threw it light as a feather into Olympus/Albuoystown canal. It sank nevertheless. For insignificant as the gesture was the relief was so enormous it turned in on itself to symbolize a state of precocity and *malaise* – equations of loss/gain – compensation of death – mathematics of grace, accent of euphoria. The stage or feather unwittingly or wittingly enlarged itself in his mind into a mountain of souls descending into sea or jungle: the housecoat of Manoa, bed and board, parrot or raven of Atlantis.

This became the game of the stone. He would return day after day, month after month, to construct his sensation. As his pebbles fell into the canal he watched the ripples expand; and always as each horizon died, he would feel a numbness at heart like a fraction in his throat whose origin fascinated him as the theorem of being. It sprang, in part, from his parents – the mother he had never seen and his father's drunken rages and sobrieties which sometimes seemed one and the same.

It was the sense of a multiplication of deaths (*stigmata of the void*) – the sense of having been part and parcel of an event akin to being born, which was yet so deeply submerged in consciousness it had no language save the spectre or map or frame imbedded in him as Victor or as "little Caesar" – the limbo dancer. It seemed absurd to say he "knew" the facts of the Caesarian operation and his mother's death. Perhaps a hint here or there let fall by his father or by a neighbour. Perhaps more than a hint since he was convinced he had heard someone say Adam had been warned his wife was unfit to bear a child and that this would entail a grave risk.

Had he heard all this or was it *malaise* or invention? As the stone descended into the canal it seemed possessed of his father's hardheartedness and his mother's apparitions: possessed of his father's tragedy in that he loved his wife but never really *felt* for her until his need of her was exposed as so great on her deathbed he saw he had unwittingly pushed her there and into the canal of oblivion where she sank: *pushed her in the name of Victor...*

All this became a vortex of sensation on OH MY – the contraction of a mirror in his side like a mathematical function. His unusual gifts at school – as Dr. Wall knew – were part compensation for this veil of childhood, veil of profanity, veil of sanctity. He was a marvel at mental arithmetic, an inbuilt "computer" – vicar of stone and flesh.

He was a marvel also at inventions – curious things – the judge's sheaf of cards – cloth, paper, cardboard, etc. Heir of El Dorado, black welder. Child of housecoat or petticoat as well. For he treasured the garment in a corner of the room which had been his mother's.

When he crawled and hid under it – to escape from his father – he was filled with a perception that dwarfed the room as if he "knew" it before he was born, limbo stone falling on his head as night fell and the fortress in which he lay was lit up by flashes of lightning: his father's presence on the other side of the cloth, profane vicar, ripple and penetration, invocation of flesh-and-blood.

Dr. Wall said it was an hallucination of the womb compounded of fear and overstimulation at the sight of Adam those nights when he hid under the petticoat and his father slept with one of his substitute women. He could hear them breathing and see them too, drunk and naked, x-ray bodies and limbs. An enormous limbo spectacle. Dance of the gods within and without their fortress of illusion.

Victor's fascination and fear became so great he sank into the measureless secret of the stone – its pyramidal strength which could reach him within his housecoat of stars and its horizons or ripples which could blaze at him with new eyes painted on rubble, marble flesh-and-blood.

This phenomenon of numbness (marble flesh-and-blood) grew into an unemotional distance between him and the scene in the room (like an artist appraising his nude model or an audience witnessing nude theatre) and made it possible for him to begin to watch the activity of substitutes like a vessel of illumination, Alias mother (starred breast), Alias father (starred phallus). It was this sensibility to unemotional ripples on the surface of space that set in motion self-made deity, blueprint of aeroplane, ship, compass, factory, cross, gaol.

Victor felt the weight of blue-print – a sense of inequality beneath the stars: a sense also of the inequality of the stars in a body of obscurity. That weight could appear at times so damning, it bred the temptation (a) to turn away from the real tasks of creative communion with sex-mask, death-mask, (b) to blast the inequality of traditions and invest in equality of conventions, browbeaten status, little Caesar, conformity, copulation of idols.

"*Dear Reader,* (THE JUDGE WROTE HALF IN THE MARGIN OF HIS BOOK AND HALF ON A VACANT CARD). My intention, in part, is to repudiate the vicarious novel – vicarious sex-mask, death-mask – where the writer, following a certain canon of clarity, claims to enter the most obscure and difficult terrain of experience without incurring a necessary burden of authenticity, obscurity or difficulty at the same time. No matter his material stems from centuries of inequality, repression, oppression, etc. All this must serve as a prophylactic in the name of emancipation or industry.

The truth is, I believe, that the novel has been conditioned for so long by comedy of manners, it overlooks an immense poetry of original and precarious features which, in fact, we can only begin to expose again by immersing ourselves in the actual difficulty of the task: by immersing ourselves in language as omen, as an equation of experience.

Wherever, therefore, in this book I or my characters speak of vicars of reality, vicar of this or that lighthouse, it is intended as a confession of abstinence – of scrupulous care, illumination rather than unexplored gloss or conscription of taste or manner upon like/unlike material.

The difficulty, of course, is one, as Rimbaud knew, few wish to confess or confront. It was he (Rimbaud) who lamented the impoverishment of Europe in a rejection of Africa and Asia. This, of course, taken at face value today in an economic surfeit and market place means little unless it is restated afresh as impoverishment in a rejection of omen, clear obscure, art/science, sacred/profane, Pacific/Atlantic the real nature, in short, factorize it as you wish, of the formidable creative task of digesting and translating our age... (THE JUDGE MADE A FEW STROKES AT THE BOTTOM OF THE CARD AND FINISHED HIS LETTER) Yours in truth, JUDGE."

He sighed and turned back from margin to mainstream: novel-vision of history.

Victor had painted the housecoat of his absent mother with stars, in one place, a pool or canal in another across which ripples fled to concentric horizons on the first or innermost ring of which (petticoat) he established the epitaph of *Child Two*.

Child One already lay under the roadway – wheel of car – and equally in the numb blueprint of Dr. Wall's surgery with arclight of the sun blazing down. As well as under the stone in the canal.

Victor was seven years' old when he drew the death of Child Two on the innermost concentric horizon of space as he felt it. This ring he called *Petticoat* (see page 84). It wasn't the wheel of a car this time but the crash of a machine he had been told of at school. Something that made him a *man* – an explorer – something that cancelled out an area of bondage… Something to do with Angel Falls and Omai Chasm where Pilot Somebody-or-Other had come down in the Bush. He (Victor) couldn't make up his mind whether to play at being that pilot (Pilot Tin) or captain of a ship or pilot of a whale (Pilot Jonah's submarine). Something to free him from *petticoat*.

The death of Child Two was for him an important horizon in this respect. It seemed to lift the weight of car and wheel off his chest and let him soar higher than he had ever dreamt in a curious chamber of time, beyond his immortal mother towards the solemn mask of a judge shielding the original blinding arclight of the sun in Dr. Wall's operating-theatre.

Victor could not make up his mind about the crash on Omai – epitaph of Child Two. It seemed, in fact, that the game of the stone possessed other alternatives and that in settling for himself as a wreck of an explorer – as brave Pilot Tin – he was merely fulfilling an equation upon the solemn mask of the arclight of the sun. An equation he called *vicar of lighthouse* or Angel of Omai.

He tried indeed to draw it on the housecoat of stars as epitaph of Child Two inscribed on petticoat but it seemed to bring him up against a wall of fire. It was like waking with the sun in one's eyes: too strong and vigorous for him to bear alone. He thought of his father and the welder's mask he wore and the furnace he carried within, stone-drunk lover. So finally – for the epitaph of Child Two on Omai – Victor drew himself as no longer within his absent mother's skin but within the demon of his father's flesh-and-blood whose brow could stand as a shield for Caesar: the mask of El Dorado.

It was a crucial departure for him – the shield or welder-mask; after that he no longer ran for shelter under the ancient petticoat. Child Three (in the wake of Epitaph Two) was born afresh from ironclad, golden father rather than cloth and fabric of mother. At first it seemed he (Child Three) had indeed acquired the vicar of lighthouse like a filtered reflex of the sun and guide-line for the future: until a charred sensation grew as well from Epitaph Two and crept into his eyes within his new shelter and claim of relief. As if he knew and felt the weight of El Dorado now, black visor, sweat of factory. For indeed in sheltering now within the mask of his father – turning the mirror of the sun there, arclight of memory – he acquired on top of a sense of numbness (phenomenon of numbness he had enjoyed in the womb of the past) a portrait of charcoal accompanying him everywhere, lines made by a tree against the horizon at sunset, the fingers of rain and dust on wall or pavement. It was a bruise he could not entirely shake off – absent immortal mother whose persistence within the brow of his father engendered a kind of scorched vision within a newly acquired moderation and freedom. Once again Victor felt the weight of blueprint – the sense of inequality not under the stars this time but within the mask of the sun.

Child Three was the submarine age – the age of the whale. In the same way that Child One had been reflected and stored in

(a) Dr. Wall's serial ghost (operation theatre);
(b) Adam's serial ghost (when the father thought the son had died under a car in the street);
(c) the stone in the canal,

so Child Three occupied a series of evolutionary premises – stable of bread, racehorses of subsistence, underground or factory.

It was the age when Victor began, in the drama of puberty, to make his circular rings (as recorded in BOOK I of this novel) around the door of the foundry. As though the mirror of appetite in his side established a vicar or vicars of lighthouse by re-tracing the concentric rings of childhood and adolescence around a father who seemed to Victor each morning, on passing through the door of the factory, to sink into a pool of labour. His re-appearance, at the end of the day, when Victor shone his mirror upon him, upon welder's brow, was the dawn of night as well as the birth of subsistence.

Dawn of night may appear a curious image but it reflected in depth Victor's fear of his father's workplace, and relief at his re-appearance before sunset. For he knew on those occasions during the day when he had ventured to approach the door of the foundry, he had been conscious of the blaze of furnaces within like a mighty engine in the bowels of a ship, and the blast in his eyes constituted for him an unbearable sunrise and the necessity for father-shield or brow. *Dawn of night.* Vicar of lighthouse.

This exposure to fire and moderation or shield against fire which his father now provided, accentuated the charcoal limbs of night. Victor traced these under the stars of ancient petticoat he no longer sheltered within as before. It was his first clear-sighted awareness of a ruined fortress – idolatrous womb – whose immanent beauty he began to extrapolate half-in-despair, half-in-tenderness. As much as to say if an artist's model could be a whore, she could also be a mother and in this confession one was involved in the deepest accents of universal complex humanity. Likewise if an artist's theme could be a cathedral, it could equally be a prison or a hospital. It was in this confrontation of opposites, these ruined prepossessions, that one glimpsed the moderation of the stone of love capable of replacing, like a Christian goal, the Gorgon classical unforgiving or unforgiven extremity – castration of hate.

It was this tenderness, imperfect human love no one can confine – beyond every profile of a perfect school or fortress of hate – that drew him to the ancient housecoat as his first revisionary canvas, artist's model: canvas and model combined: like a tattoo he had seen lovingly executed on one of the limbo dancers, sailorboy of Albuoystown.

He was, at that moment, already in process of making Epitaph Three (horizon of the whale). Something blackened – dawn of night – upon which or through which he glimpsed the uncharted seas beyond both whale and rose whose evolution lay not only in intricate vastness of design but vast intricacy of storehouses of light (whalebone or petal). Glimpsed the rose which lay upon a further concentric horizon (Epitaph Four). Epitaph Three which he was now in process of making, resembled a tattoo upon mother and rose like a tree of charcoal. It was a way of investing in the bride of the sea, a wife in every port, as though the sailorboy of Albuoystown went down into the mother of his ship for the last time as into the immortal roots of darkness to carve there upon bone and petal his own black unremembered kith and kin.

Victor's immersion in constructing the tree of night was symbolic of spaces – sea, land, air: uncharted seas upon which the drama of puberty visualized half-obscurely, half-clearly, all the concentric horizons of the stone – petticoat, whale, rose, iron mask, parrot, raven, baboon, madonna (see page 84).

It was an immersion which carried the accents of a croak as well as a song, choirboy and adolescent, the breaking voices of childhood and manhood; the young sailor of Albuoystown may well have been the flesh of a dream whose stories thrilled the imagination of the boy as deeply as reports of explorer (Pilot Tin) in Omai Chasm: stories of adventures in many lands and seas all (Victor felt later in retrospect) moving irresistibly to the day of the Strike, the act of sabotage and the burning of his own home – bed and board.

The judge may well have been the flesh of a dream looking down from parrot and raven perched on his shoulders.

Baboon and Madonna may well have been the serial ghosts of whale and rose within a complex nurse of identity.

ADVENTURES OF THE SAILOR

"Dear Posterity (WROTE DR. WALL ADDRESSING A BLANK CARD IN JUDGE'S PACK),

In entering upon the adventures of the sailor may I attempt to revive your interest in the vicar of lighthouse. For, in fact, it is the quest of the lighthouse which is native to the arts of the sailor of Albuoystown.

If you and I should ever meet (which is unlikely) you will come face to face with me (not only in operating theatres) but in derelict courtrooms; ancient waiting-rooms, constellations, warehouses, wharves, streetlamps at the corner of nowhere, projections and maps, *bric-à-brac* of the dead, pyramids: all in a sense expressive of *ruin*. Not 'ruin' in the given sense of the word – something finished, sad, bankrupt, though this may be a suffering aspect of it. But *ruin* as a confession of otherness, a vision of otherness, something numinous and transparent through which we move – conscious of our lapses and imperfections – towards the supra-personal, the transcendental.

Ruin, in this sense, is a unique witness of an ultimate digestion within space of unequal features and factors – not digestion in gross, personalistic, individualistic figures – but digestion upon a scale of balances that subsists *through* disintegration not *upon* disintegration. The distinction is an enormous one. Those who build *upon* disintegration seek – wittingly or unwittingly – to bury the past in fortresses of self-deception. Those – on the other hand – who articulate a certain feeling for mass or structure *through* disintegration seek the light of compensation in everything they do: an ideal balance which, in the nature of things, is the frailest but most enduring spirit of art in that it moves within and beyond one's grasp to balance *loss* with *gain*, conquered with conqueror, destroyed with destroyer, unmade with made. It is this infinite tormenting theorem of inspiration that corresponds across space – through epitaphs of space – to a sacramental vacancy/ruin: vicar of lighthouse.

Earlier in this book I was accused of seeking to balance primitive *fetish* with Christian *omen*.

Such a balance takes us far afield indeed across and through many horizons into old worlds and new. For example the first vessel Sailor joined was called *Osiris*. You may recall that Osiris became known as the 'mummy with the long member'. I am reminded of Darwin's theory of the ornament: too much of a good thing. (See page 60 where Darwin speaks of the horns of beetles. I am reminded at this juncture that Osiris was also called 'the scarab with a phallus'.)

And, in fact, the scale of the Osiris myth may appear to some as a posthumous scandal. Something *News of the Globe* would pick up with relish if it could be given a fashionable twist. With his dead member he (Osiris) is reputed to have impregnated a living woman. And one is involved here *either* in an excessive mythological ornament, prophylactic robot (which is what it may seem to many) *or* (as it may seem to a few) in a remarkable omen signifying the barren living (feuds of the living) and the fertile dead, a metaphysical projection into the future of indestructible mankind despite suffocating hordes of tyranny, even genocide, through a vicar of lighthouse.

The point to note is that Osiris had been dismembered and the process of assembling his parts in the most grotesque particulars is a fundamental paradox. To conscript the ruined dismembered god upon a new material base could reflect the absurdity of the ornament – of both life and death. Or it could reflect *through* the illumination of the body – a density and transparency that brings into focus the torment of divided power, evil and good, the fortress of the soul, the terrifying genius of man to *see* though *blind,* hear though deaf, feel though unfelt.

It is instructive in this context to compare Osiris with Christ. The body of Christ has never been located. According to the records it vanished completely. And it is this *vacancy or corridor* of Christ that helps us – if we see it in a certain light –

to approach 'the mummy with the long member' as *omen* rather than material base, omen of indestructibility, omen of continuity rather than monument of absurdity. This *rapport* between *fetish* and *omen,* I submit, ornament and vision, is the true vicar of lighthouse whose ramifications into the past (pre-history) and into the future (post-idolatry) we need to investigate with the greatest care.

Yours mythically,

ALIAS WALL."

The sailor stopped. He had been reading the above letter to Victor and a crowd of limbo bystanders with a wry, twisted face, idiom of charcoal.

"Tell me about Rose," Alias Copper said, reflecting the sun like a kitchen utensil upon Adam. "Mummy with the long member indeed."

"I have a letter from her too," said the sailor. "Translation of charcoal. Forgive the sketchiness and crudeness too. As you see it's black. Still a rose is a rose is a rose. A fire is a rose is charcoal is a rose. It was the time when I was reported drowned."

"Drunk you mean," said Copper. Somebody sniggered.

"Dear Sailor (WROTE ROSE),

Last night I saw the *Osiris* in harbour and went down to inquire for you. I was told you were dead – drowned off the Orinoco. Missing they said. Almost certainly dead. I cannot describe to you how numb and confused I felt – as if I felt (what madness) I no longer felt at all. You see from this my numbness and state of confusion. I would have cheerfully split my head on a stone or a wall to bring you back. Yes – that's how everything seemed – a stone or a wall one implored. I blundered into carcass after carcass, rumshop after rumshop, rotten cinema after cinema, looking for a ghost.

I remembered you once said to me by way of a joke that you had a wife in every port. And I – recalling that – set out deliberately to fertilize my grief, endure my loss – by constructing something in myself, all women to all men: the wife in every port.

I know what you'll think when I say this: she picked up a crude devil of a man on the waterfront to sleep with. The cruder and longer the better. Anything to make her *feel* she didn't feel any more.

But you're wrong. That wasn't how it was. I picked up a man, yes. He had just come out of hospital. Had been knifed in a fight two months before by Tarantula. You remember Tarantula, don't you? Omai dancer. When I picked him up I thought he was drunk. But he wasn't really. He had been drinking but he wasn't drunk. You know what I mean. Infected and inoculated. You've been like that many a time. Delirious like the shaking limbs of a beacon, dance of the waves which lives through the old quarrel, the old feud between night and day, land and water. You would think his old slashed electric head had fallen to the guillotine of Albuoystown – basket of space. Or that he had been fused and kicked into Carnival.

When I touched him he looked at me and called me Rose. Perhaps he had seen me somewhere or sometime before. But it was the way he said it: as if I was someone new. A dancing portrait through a portrait. It may have been the streetlamp of Albuoystown. Sometimes it makes me look gaudy, painted and vile. But in his eyes that night the light was different. Transparent like a veil on which the most delicate colours had been drawn, transubstantiation of spider. A kind of ritual abstemiousness as though on the threshold of sex there are spirits involved whose organs are etched and burnt into an invisible waltz. Ruin and yet co-ordination of singing wires, telegraph of the senses – of the ages.

You know what I mean. After that comes the first intense preoccupation with charcoal – postmortem fire, something vast and immanent in that it crumbles and yet restores itself like a tree which shoots up in an instant, extrapolates itself in all directions, branches, trunk, leaves, blossom, flower – all miraculously sustained by, as it were, drenching the fire, holding it still, still as the dance of death, fertile as the ramifications of a dark mirror through which the fire has passed yet in which the fire remains like a diamond, in concert with seam and charcoal.

These, shall I say, are but equations of light. Equations of the dance. Omai tarantula. Soon – shall I say – the deadly thing happens. Vomit of insecurity. Violated like a sack on the waterfront. In bed. Bed and board. And it is here that the colours begin to run. And as they melt this time the earlier distinction goes, ritual song, drenched fire – only the shock remains that what one has been involved in is not *fire*, is not *music*. Is not *you*, Sailor, is not the one I truly need. It's a hoax of a man that I have been nursing: a sick man who has been nursing me, in turn, a dying woman. All we can salvage from it now is that, on the scale of love to which we danced, we glimpsed the victor of death in spite of ourselves, in spite of our climax of disillusion, by feeling the weight of our non-feeling in the end as a crime against the frail origins of man – of all mankind.

Victor of death. There, in fact, lay my son and heir. Not mine alone. But all women's. All wives in all ports. Pregnant that night we all were. For a man we never saw again. Never wanted possibly to see again. He had founded our vicarage – vicarage of the lighthouse – hostel of the waterfront.

I had swallowed him as the sea swallowed you, Sailor. And when he left I began to rock myself to sleep like the cradle of being. *I needed you.* You seemed then so much larger than life. Large as a death which could support a constitution of dread, monster as well as divine. *It was a way, shall I say, of hanging on to life when I thought there was nothing to live for.* A way of nursing my innermost original resources, however incomprehensible, some may say, however frail – nursing you back, Sailor, Victor of death, to life…

ROSE"

112

PROSECUTING COUNSEL: Monologue. This novel/vision/ defence/letter of yours is monologue. How can Rose address Sailor as Victor?

DEFENCE COUNSEL: Not monologue. Dialogue.

PROSECUTING COUNSEL: Dialogue with whom?

DEFENCE COUNSEL: Eternity.

PROSECUTING COUNSEL *(laughs):* That's absurd. Very funny indeed. Dialogue with eternity! *Doppelgänger.* How goddamned absurd can you get? Nobody believes in anybody's ghost nowadays. Social escapism is what counts, something that can be patented in the name of separate, solid fisticuffs.

DEFENCE COUNSEL *(with the air of a postman in a black/white comedy, sacred heresy, who confesses to a robot/raven, in an age before pigeon, before Reuter):* I operate from the standpoint of one and agent: wired to eternity.

PROSECUTING COUNSEL *(pityingly):* You're stark, staring... drunk... or mad... or both...

DEFENCE COUNSEL *(to parrot on judge's shoulder):* One and agent are steeped in density/transparency which is, in fact, a way of saying these are equations of time: dead and living time. Dead time is stored energy which may have a catastrophic explosive significance (in terms of overlong repression, depression, oppression); living time is that power or medium of presence one can summon at any stage to commune with and compensate the past.

PROSECUTING COUNSEL *(staring balefully at Reuter's pigeon, Manoa's parrot, prehistoric raven):* I take it that your witnesses are "structurally" there within a certain legacy or stage... wired to eternity, pantheon of the post.

DEFENCE COUNSEL: My witnesses reflect the consolation or desolation of time: a constructive mystery in that each unique desert or horizon still fulfils a remarkable purpose in overcoming a certain illusion – self-sufficient illusion of character. It is this uniqueness of the limited person/

113

postmaster in a desert of communication that is a truer reflex of the need of man – the emergency of art and science – since as agencies, one of the other, they stand within a mirror reflecting and reflected beyond their station, subsistent upon dread as well as grace, darkness as well as light, discrete yet translated into community. They begin to learn, as it were, that the spectre of time is something they cannot conscript whatever stamp or seal they manufacture.

PROSECUTING COUNSEL: You're a rum kid. Rum charcoal.

(Sailor stopped speaking. He was stripped to the waist: immensely tattooed: whalebone and rose: he had been reading the rough draft of a play to his limbo audience at the bottom of the sea which Victor had sketched in charcoal upon the housecoat of stars).

And now began the dance of Sailor and Rose at the bottom of the sea – a vast serial feature of the drama of puberty within which Victor began to visualize an extended freedom from the petticoat of mother (idolatrous fixation and womb), an independent confrontation with father through crumbling mask, sweat of fire.

The submarine character of the dance (as Dr. Wall knew it) was an intimate re-structuring of those early scenes – overstimulation, limbo sex – when his father used to bring a woman into the room and Victor, three to five years old, would hide under the housecoat in the corner to escape from them. Perhaps it was all some curious dream within which it was forgotten he existed at all and in the half-darkness of space, stone-drunk limbs of man and woman assumed a profound regression and constellation, pre-natal vessel.

His emergence from the hallucination of violation within pregnant mother came paradoxically enough with a growing appetite for emotion. Appetite for fire. For waking, as it were, with the blaze of the sun in his eyes, he sought as his shield the father-brow of subsistence. And inoculated by fire, insulated from fire, he began with the charcoal of memory – epitaphs and stages – to adumbrate, from an unconscious/ subconscious struggle with fate, a deeper and more far-reaching processional note of liberation.

At the climax of puberty, the horizons of stone (petticoat, whale, rose, iron mask, parrot, raven, baboon, madonna) were instinct with the brood of catastrophe, whether in the form of regression once again into the mother or sabotage in the future by the father: but precisely because of this uncanny illumination within potencies of disaster, it was possible to gain a timely residue or mirror of sensation through which to extrapolate and reflect an advance guard or maturity of vision. Vicar of lighthouse. Sailor and Rose.

SAILOR (*whom Victor has sketched as one of his heroes on the housecoat of stars*): The first dance of Sailor and Rose – one day you'll be a sailor, won't you, Victor, or will it be a welder or a porknocker or a soldier or a judge (*laughs*) – is called the Iron Mask. I used to work on a ship called the *Iron Mask* you see.

VICTOR (*writes 'Iron Mask' on petticoat*): Dumas.

SAILOR: Yes, it's the dance of the true king imprisoned in the dungeon of the sun at the midnight bottom of the sea. But dispossessed as he is, he begins to turn the tables on apparent victor or twin (*winks at Victor*) by writing into creation something it has been claimed has never been done – the signature of the true victim or king – king of creation.

VICTOR: But he's masked, Sailor, he's gloved and masked in my sketch. It's like a faceless thing without name or reason. How can he write anything at all?

SAILOR: It seems incredible, I know, you've put him at a considerable disadvantage, but you see the most incredible of incredible things has happened to the king of creation – he's dispossessed and he's learnt the arts of dispossession. You must let this sink into your head,

115

Victor, if you want to help him help you to be free. For therethrough – through his dispossession – he is enabled to enter into the innermost secret locks and prisons and chains of exiled/imprisoned mankind. He knows what slavery is all about – from the inside, see? He dances through the backdoor, as it were, anywhere and everywhere: the sea, the watershed/chasm/jungle of Omai… Call it by any universal name. This is his innermost theme and function, the celebration of freedom *through* knowing unfreedom. One has to seek it differently in each age. It always comes from outside/in since whether you see it or not it's already inside/out – dispossessed.

VICTOR: Charcoal?

SAILOR: Call it charcoal if you wish, Victor. Charcoal signature. Once it was called Eden (the age of pubertan Adam, stamp of stone); at another time something else, maybe Atlantis (the age of Prometheus, brand of fire); at another time still Mosquito or Manoa (the age of gold, sting of Albuoystown) and so on. Now it's this blackness – nigredo – like a cave painting at midnight, stamp of dawn, dungeon of the sun, dawn of night – that carries the original sacrament of relationships (dispossession/freedom). You see, Victor, this dance – the dance of sailor and rose as I have christened it – celebrates the alternatives that lie before you, within you: as both victor and victim: celebrates the innermost palette of unfreedom/freedom, creative necessity, paradox of paradoxes, logic of catastrophe, dispossessed original godhead. Therefore, you see, when Rose and I dance, we celebrate the bottomless resources of divinity extrapolated into our age, our limbs. For we know it's idle to traffic in substitutes like apartheid or violence once you've been seared by the real thing long long ago as we were with our king, residual function of fire, inoculation/insulation/, charcoal of the psyche. Rose of midnight.

"Rose of midnight," Victor wrote on the prison of the stone as it sank into the sea. Pre-historic cave or lighthouse or tomb. Cave painting of eternity. Sea-mask, sex-mask, death-mask, life-mask, unicorn, magician. Catastrophe of catastrophes. Bottomless resources of divinity. The scale, advance guard vision of maturity, was so fantastic and enormous it energized the signature of creation in the dance of history . . . vacancy or corridor. The most delicate fluid stamp of origins (call it grace, call it infinite darkness-in-light, infinite light-in-darkness).

As the stone sank it acquired a numinous capacity, collision brow of the ages, explosive architecture: it acquired limits of expansion, expansion of limits, disintegration, integration, ornamentation, idiosyncrasy to maintain or find a capacity beyond capacities for endless sovereign resourcefulness in unlocking the prisonhouse of the ages.

PARROT (*reading Victor's lines from judge's shoulder*): Some may think, Sailor, you're charting a manifesto for promiscuity, even violence, revolution, in spite of your protestations to the contrary.

SAILOR (*turning his mask up to the ceiling of time*): Ignorant armies will clash by night... I know...

PARROT (*mockingly*): In your name I suppose?

SAILOR: Therein lies the heart of the trouble. Until an age comes to terms with its claustrophic name, finds an equation of dispossession – an equation of sovereign catastrophe which is already *there* in point of fact – happened long long ago and needs a creative vision and application in each age, creative translation for this age – until it can do that, it will continue to invest in substitute catastrophes (violence is a substitute, I cannot say it often enough) and will postpone coming to grips with the creative tasks of freedom through unfreedom...

RAVEN (*looping the loop*): Do you mean, Sailor, that this is an age of the uncreative?

SAILOR (*unlooping the loop, dance of the cliché of catastrophe*): Age of the uncreative, yes, in spite of all the inventions. We're slaves to industry. Slaves to factory. Slaves to monotony. Slaves to desk. Slaves to fortune. It's ironic but because we believe in the heights of the banal and overlook the depths of royalty (dispossessed claim) we lose a vocation for freedom, for originality. We don't even know it when we see it. We want the ready-made comparison.

PARROT (*crowning the cliché*): I know a clean cage when I see it. Nothing's wrong with technology. I like to be stuffed with domesticity myself, I like to be stuffed with security.

RAVEN (*croaks on judge's shoulder*): At a price.

SAILOR (*traces with the thorn of the rose*): At a price, yes, the raven is right. And the price should carry a real endorsement of vocation. For security, in our age, is merely the bauble of dispossession, a toy of the manufacturers of unfreedom…

RAVEN (*traces with the claw of memory*): … of slavery in which we are unwittingly immersed: whereas we should be profoundly critical, creatively active… .

PARROT (*traces with the beak of reflection*): … in order to express the unique dilemmas of sensibility in our time. For to be profoundly critical, creatively active, is all the more imperative, in the circumstances of today, if we are to translate, within an original lighthouse, the dispossession of the king. Black king of history.

JUDGE POLISHES OFF SKETCHES OF DÉCOR, CLAW, BEAK, LANDSCAPE OF TIME, THEATRE OF COURTROOM, DANCE OF THE CLICHÉS OF CATASTROPHE.

BOOK III

OMAI

I am one
who as in innocent play sought out his guilt,
And now through guilt seeks other innocence.
                                    EDWIN MUIR

9

DANCE OF THE STONE

The descent of the stone in its multiple generation, ageless deity, drew into orbit several movements or horizons, the first of which (popularly called petticoat) has been previously executed in this novel by the limbo band of Albuoystown, namely

Page 38; dance of the petticoat, cloud in trousers.

"Victor was three years old when the traumatic *caveat,* psychological shape-changing premises began. *A man and a woman were cohabiting on the floor.* Urban stomach – nightmare. Rotting boarding-house. Single room. Congestion. Poverty. Art of the slums. Spectral intestines. Sometimes one elbow to a family of ten. He could see them clearly (or was it confusedly): the chasm of her thighs. A cloud like trousers draped over rock.

Victor cried. The man reached up. Veiled form on the other side of the globe. Gave him a clout: inside. 'BUGGER THE CHILD OF AGES,' he whispered and cried. 'QUIET. *PLEASE.'* Poked him in the side: inside. Spear of the clown. *Dreamt of them now as if he were inside, still waiting to be born, on the other side of the globe, inside the man, inside the woman.* Misty figures. Shape-changing. Shape-shifting. Leaps and bounds. Spectral flesh. Grotesque clown. Limbo side, spear in his side. Like a phantom dancer under a mile-stone, limbo dancer, cross and spear, arched door.

Never knew his mother. Died when he was born. A voluminous petticoat hanging on the wall was all that remained to speak of her. Subsistence of memory. Victor curled himself up there, protective skin, memory's dress. His father was drunk. Boxing Day. The room was a shambles. Victor remained hidden there (within the petticoat) until it was safe to emerge: crawled on the floor towards a window. Twentieth-century window. It was raining outside. Raining blood. Global civil war. Insurrection Day. He could hear the drums on the road – lightning and thunder – the rowdy band of Albuoystown. He pulled himself up – *there they were*: rowdy elements, descendants of 'free' men and 'slaves'. Apocrypha of the living and the dead. Insurrection womb and race. Dance of ironical victor and victim. Strong ageless women dancing on stilts in waistcoat and trousers (high up – off the ground – in the sky); and great limbo men in striped drawers and dresses sliding under a bar. Limbo bar. Inverse location of sex. Door of rebirth. Sanctification of otherness."

SECOND MOVEMENT

The second movement or horizon of the dance of the stone (popularly called whale) has also been previously adumbrated in this novel as a multiple epitaph – Victor/Adam, judge, Rose, namely (a) the whale of technology/ mythology, (b) the whale of mythology/technology, (c) the whale of grief, Sailor/Rose.

(a) *Page 45; dance of the clouds, Warehouse Sky (Wall)*.

"It gave him (as he waited for his father to come) a view of the river, white, beaten gold at first, turning magnificently and slowly into scarlet lion, bronze child, cloud, sailing-vessel, fishing-craft, rocking-tub under a feather. A whale of a steamer began to appear – double-decker of sunset. Still no sign of his father."

(b) *Page 93; dance of aeroplane/ Manoa*.

"The judge glanced at the sky from the window of his aeroplane and shuffled his deck of cards. He could see far below him in the mist of the late afternoon what looked like the spirit of a town, settlement or harbour, whale of a ship lit from stem to stern sailing beneath the clouds across parrot's ocean or peacock's wave: flying fish of El Dorado. It reminded him of his own phantasmagoric sketches, illuminated rainbow of night, the night Adam had set fire to the factory, grown berserk, run through Albuoystown to his own home where he burnt bed and board."

(c) *Page 112; dance of the sea-Rose.*

"I had swallowed him as the sea swallowed you, Sailor. And when he left I began to rock myself to sleep like the cradle of being. *I needed you.* You seemed then so much larger than life. Large as a death which could support a constitution of dread, monster as well as divine. *It was a way, shall I say, of hanging on to life when I thought there was nothing to live for.* A way of nursing my innermost original resources, however incomprehensible, some may say, however frail – nursing you back, Sailor, Victor of death, to life…"

THIRD MOVEMENT

The third movement or horizon of the dance of the stone (popularly called Iron Mask) has also been previously adumbrated in this novel as (see page 115) – "this uncanny illumination within potencies of disaster (in order) to gain a timely residue or mirror of sensation through which to extrapolate and reflect an advance guard or maturity of vision…"

FOURTH AND FIFTH MOVEMENTS

The fourth and fifth movements of the dance of the stone (popularly called parrot and raven) have also been adumbrated in this novel as complex heralds of the landscape of time –

Pages 90-91; the Calendar.

"This, in fact, had a close bearing on the judge's novel in that his choice of forty years was a symbolic equivalent to the Mexican cycle of fifty-two years. Also the judge's cards and sketches were a symbolic equivalent to the Mexican sheaf of time, series of time which bore a correspondence to one of spades, two of hearts, three of diamonds, four of clubs, five of spades, six of hearts, seven of diamonds, eight of clubs, etc. Again the judge's indeterminate sets and colours, parrot, raven, rose, etc. were a symbolic equivalent to the ancient Mexican calendar – rabbits, reeds, flints, houses.

There was, however, a profound distinction the judge wished to imply in his vision of time *vis-à-vis* the ancient Mexican obsession with a sheaf or game. The distinction was an important one. It could be stated in this way: the Mexicans – precisely because they wished to conscript time on a material base – were drawn every fifty-two years by their fear that time had to be manufactured afresh (the game needed to commence afresh) or it would slip from their grasp forever.

Thus they seized on a victim – on flesh-and-blood as their fortress or factory of time – and tore the living heart out as from a rabbit, stuffed rabbit. Then by firing this base they greeted the bank of the sun as a new dawn, newly-minted time.

The judge, on the other hand, precisely because he wished a qualitative illumination to emerge in his novel history rather than a quantitative bank of time, saw – beforehand – into the unique density and transparency of his victim (spectral character and dust) and refrained therefore from inflicting a senseless ordeal on what was in essence the ghost of the universe, serial participation in time, universal subsistence of memory…"

SIXTH AND SEVENTH MOVEMENTS OF THE
DANCE OF THE STONE:
BABOON AND MADONNA

As the plane flew towards OH MY the judge was intent on a sketch which he entitled *Alternatives:* a sketch-within-a-sketch-within-a-sketch: Sailor, Welder, Porknocker, Judge, Pilot. Within the climax of puberty these careers lay before Victor as before the perennial child in the judge who dreams of becoming an engine driver or an astronaut depending on the rage of the day: the first explosive shudders of longing and ambition begin to shake the entire subconscious/conscious fabric of existence.

As the judge thought of Victor a train of memory ran through him like an electric signal. What was, in many so-called normal cases, a dormant fire became for Victor capital residue when his father burnt bed and board.

As though a great column of smoke arose within which he sank like a stone, vanished from sight. *It was one of the most distressing features of the case the judge recalled after forty years. The disappearance of Adam's son the very day sentence was passed. Ran away from home. Never seen or heard of again apart from Dame Rumour.* It had, in fact, turned with the judge into the theme of a lifetime: an exploration of the alarm bell of puberty.

Some said Victor ran away to sea upon *Osiris* – an Egyptian vessel – as a cabin boy. Others that it was *The Iron Mask* which he sailed upon and which sank in a storm off the Orinoco. It was known that Victor's father had friends on board who may have taken pity on the boy.

There were other rumours that he turned stowaway and was successfully smuggled into the United States where he sold newspapers, went to school, worked during vacation, graduated in law and was elected judge of the courts of America. (One of the idiosyncratic dreams of his court was that everyone followed another convention and addressed him as *my lord* as a mark of respect for that other judge who had sentenced his father the day he (Victor) ran off to take the law too in a noble stride).

There were other rumours that – apart from portrait-within-portrait, judge-within-judge – he wrote poems and novels after many years at sea which won him a peculiar reputation for canons of obscurity, and that he returned to South America and disappeared in the Bush – on the watershed of Omai – in search of a claim Adam had established there on his release from prison.

In the present work – the pages of which he shuffled on his lap – the judge dreamt that he (Victor) was engaged in writing his last novel *through* him – medium of presence, crashed aeroplane.

It was an obsession or preoccupation that dogged him in one form or another from the day he sentenced the boy's father: dogged him in the shape of rumours of other jurisdictions, modern and ancient, the lost claim and the found, a court-within-a-court-within-a-court. The first day he learnt – in the week sentence was passed – of Victor's disappearance, he was stricken by enigma, guilt and innocence, face of a child, stubborn, black, face of all men in flight from the womb. One was inclined to take it for granted, he knew, that a child was heard and not seen at one stage, seen and not heard later. Like a prisoner in the dock whose heart-beat is his voice, a portrait on the wall whose colours stifle their cry.

The judge recalled reading somewhere that in a child's life the prenatal "trial or experience" was more subtle and far-reaching than most people wanted to understand. Also the years from three to five were a storehouse of the deepest impressions whose momentum and significance were all the greater for their lack of expression, their void of language. The approaches to puberty and puberty itself (say ten to fourteen) were symbolic too in a depth of apprehension within which all the variables and possibilities that lay in the past and future germinated or froze, became for some a source of eternal embarrassment (ruined godhead), for others the ground of unbroken adolescence (caged godhead). For others still an embarkation within a precarious vessel upon the sea of maturity, sea of humanity.

This was the last time, the judge-within-a-judge knew, he would write in the name of Victor/Adam. His attempts before had been rejected as obscure because he refused to impose a false coherency upon material one had to digest – perhaps all one's life – to begin to find in degrees of peculiar authenticity, a true groping equation in art or language to the fundaments of existence *through* history or the void which was native to history.

It was not his object to exploit his material within a monolithic cast or mould, sentiment or callous, enchantment or substitute. These exploitations were better left to intellectuals – and he was not an intellectual in any given predictable fashion or creed. He was a creative struggler who, in the actual task of being born through words, *saw* – as upon a strange land of primordial/broken vessels – signposts he had either forgotten or had never seen before.

In this respect the struggle was also a voyage – a real sometimes inextricably woven series of adventures, painful and horrifying. But always profoundly true, profoundly necessary since it was a quest for authentic correspondences with the chained soul, the soul of the child, the silent portrait on the wall he had once been long long ago.

And this was the reason why earlier in this novel he had tried to establish the significance of omen, celebration *through* the inarticulate: the discovery of a voice related to omen: language as omen in spite of or *through* ruin and rhetoric. And thus in speaking of *hypnosis* (Dr. Wall's theme) it was his intention to plumb – beyond a mass substitute – a significant buried awareness of community, fragmentation and wholeness, within which – if we were attentive enough – shone the organ of consciousness – vicar of lighthouse.

Perhaps he was wrong about all this. Civilization wasn't sick – it was hilarious and funny. To hell with the celebration of hidden resources, to heaven with robot and overt prophylactic.

Time to shut up. This was his last novel. If he lived for another hour, day, year, century – in his flight to OH MY – *these pages must serve as his epitaph*. It was, in short, the end of his life as public poet or witness on behalf of a private victim in courtroom or void.

The judge shuffled his sketches and cards. There stood Victor within schooldoor marked prospects and futures: alternatives.

Shuffled his sketches again. There – thought the judge – stands primary mask and clown, scholar: life-mask, death-mask. Born during World War I in a British Colony on the coastlands of South America. Steeped in the three R's. One foot in two M's (mathematics and mythology), the other in a single L (Latin) – residual functions of Pythagoras and Homer, Caesar and Hannibal.

Shuffled his sketches again. One hand on an expurgated series, English history and literature. The other on limbo pavement – East Indian/African folk tales, stories of porknocker/sailor/welder/El Dorado, charcoal limbs, artists' wall in the marketplace.

There he was – Sailor/Victor – washed ashore upon ancient pavement as if, for him, the new world on which he had been drawn was still unborn – hallucinated womb of the gods. Yet unborn as it was, the birth of memory presided there to confirm violence or death – death by drowning, misadventure, war, suicide, knife, tarantula – as another substitute, another portrait of innermost conviction, inner most sacrifice in the name of conqueror/conquered whose light could still be garnered into extrapolative design – vicar of freedom.

Another substitute, another portrait indeed – the judge reflected – glancing along the sea of clouds outside the window of his aeroplane to the distant horizon of Omai where it wasn't Sailor/Victor he saw now but Victor/Adam under a sky still blazing like hypnotic fire: silver pavement, gold pavement, sulphur pavement, continent or heartland washed by a sea of cloud.

And here unlike Sailor/Victor who had forgotten the free world and dreamt it had never been born, Victor/Adam had forgotten every ancient *caveat* within newborn bias of opinion, within material claim of Adam, within material claim of the son-in-the-father.

The judge sighed, reflecting on his own material bias at this juncture, his own opinionated furies from the year of the trial. It was the first time, balancing Sailor/Victor against Victor/Adam, that he felt both descent and ascent beyond the chasm of adventure, sea of Mosquito, mask of El Dorado: a pavement of time whose self-evident bias and relief put into a new light the crucifixion of memory. He was now in a true position to feel the rough edges upon the smooth lie of death: something that could prick his fingers for the first sharp indelible time like omen or rose (the blood of Christ), splinter his prejudices for the first true time like lens or distortion (the science of spirit).

And it was here, in truth, that the ground of alternatives one sought to expose through self-division acquired an activity beyond the dawn of night...

...The figure of the baboon drawn on the pavement of the sky now held Victor in her arms in the jungle of the sea against the aeroplane. It was as if clouds of earth and sky on the ridge of Omai became a remarkable kind of sentient waxworks: waxworks of the baboon.

She nursed him back to life, drowned sailor, wreck, explorer, child. Drew him to her breasts, black moons, pavement, crossed by the flute of the sun, hollow tree, pavement, crossed by the flute of the bone. *Boom, boom* of the sea, drawn there on the pavement like a shell, gun, aeroplane in the sky. The judge twisted his ventilator, fortress of the ape.

Had he dreamt it (Pilot Tin) the instant he collided? Had he tasted it (Adam) the instant he burnt (never intended to burn) bed and board ? Had he felt it (Victor) the instant he flashed his mirror, mirror of appetite?

Pavement of the ape. He drew on his scorched bed, board, scorched earth, wave, scorched air, pavement – the clichés of catastrophe.

As though, having died one time, the second, third, fourth, fifth, etc. became successively easier, and now he could confront with the profoundest equipment of all the waxworks of the baboon, waxworks of cloud, crucifixion of memory as it bled, heraldic fire, pavement fire, gargoyle of fire, child of fire: *the death of Child Three* (see pages 103-104 for Child One and Child Two) *the night Adam burnt bed and board.*

Victor remembered clearly waking in his bed, charcoal petticoat, housecoat on fire. As it blazed he was stricken by the curious sensation of a constellated arm reaching out for the last time towards him from ancestral cover, bearing him up for the last time (hallucinated cradle) before it crumbled, flesh-and-blood pavement, mother, baboon.

Often he had hidden there beneath it from the wrath of father but now – dawn of night – it pushed him out for the last time, swam with him but pushed him out across the sea of Omai for the last time – flamed with him but pushed him up to the ridge of OH MY for the last time – flew with him but pushed him on in his flight to Omai for the last time. Alternatives of cliché, cliché of catastrophe, death/life by land, sea and air – all woven together in a spectre of time – face of the clock – as if the fire of time began to blaze in his father's head and he (Victor) found himself dragged from bed, pushed across the room, pushed out of doors on to the street wreathed in smoke, arms of the baboon, ancient cloud, ancient mother drawn there on the pavement of the folk. A burning child from whom a supernatural extension of alternatives fled like sparks across an entire continent, pavement of the globe, fire-engine of adolescence, infinite charcoal, heart of love.

As the judge glanced across the pavement of Manoa, the fire-engine of love gathered momentum, aeroplane. He could see Victor, child of dawn, dawn of night, in the thick bustling throng of the clouds as hoses were turned on burning bed and board: his eyes fixed in a wall of faces, sea of faces, ridge of faces. As the last flickering beams of El Dorado subsided Adam, too, stood there on the horizon of dreams.

Victor turned and saw him, amazed to find his father had been engaged in fighting the blaze, the very blaze he had started. Originator of the fire. Mask of function: mask of emotion. His face on the pavement was grained and dark, his hands too gloved in cloud. Victor stared. He was dressed in rags, trousers in cloud, but most astonishing of all was the ragged petticoat he had unwittingly acquired going back and forth into the blaze of the sun.

It was the last time Victor was to see the remnants of that ancient housecoat, housecoat of stars, epitaph of Child Three. It lay there now across his father's breast like a shield and an omen of godhead: the godhead in the man: the man in the godhead: ultimate sacrifice: ultimate sentence: ultimate forgiveness.

Victor blew – breath of wind – upon it. It crumbled, very slowly, across the pavement, very majestically. His faint breath lifted it, expunged it of fear, of loss, of degradation, of extinction of species, so that – in conformity with the very ruin of catastrophe – it retained a living spark, a frail star, star of the Madonna.

ABOUT THE AUTHOR

Wilson Harris was born in 1921 in New Amsterdam in British Guiana, with a background which embraces African, European and Amerindian ancestry. He attended Queen's College between 1934-1939, thereafter studying land surveying and beginning work as a government surveyor in 1942, rising to senior surveyor in 1955. In this period Harris became intimately acquainted with the Guyanese interior and the Amerindian presence. Between 1945-1961, Harris was a regular contributor of stories, poems and essays to *Kyk-over-Al* and part of a group of Guyanese intellectuals that included Martin Carter, Sidney Singh and Ivan Van Sertima. His first publication was a chapbook of poems, *Fetish*, (1951) under the pseudonym Kona Waruk, followed by the more substantial *Eternity to Season* (1954) which announced Harris's commitment to a cross-cultural vision in the arts, linking the Homeric to the Guyanese. Harris's first published novel was *Palace of the Peacock* (1960), followed by a further 23 novels with *The Ghost of Memory* (2006) as the most recent. His novels comprise a singular, challenging and uniquely individual vision of the possibilities of spiritual and cultural transcendence out of the fixed empiricism and cultural boundedness that Harris argues has been the dominant Caribbean and Western modes of thought.

Harris has written some of the most suggestive Caribbean criticism in *Tradition the Writer and Society* (1967), *Explorations* (1981) and the *Womb of Space* (1983), commenting on his own work, the limitations of the dominant naturalistic mode of Caribbean fiction, and the work of writers he admires such as Herman Melville.

Following the breakdown of his first marriage, Harris left Guyana for the UK in 1959. He married the Scottish writer Margaret Burns and settled in Chelmsford. Thereafter, until his retirement, Wilson Harris was much in demand as visiting professor and writer in residence at many leading universities.

Wilson Harris was knighted in 2010. He died in March 2018.

Heartland
ISBN: 9781845230968; pp. 96; pub. 2009; £7.99
With an introduction by Michael Mitchell.

Zechariah Stevenson, son of a wealthy businessman, is the
watchman at a timber grant deep in the Guyanese interior. In
flight from the scandal of a fraud and the connected disappearance of his mistress, Stevenson isolates himself in the forest,
which he discovers is disturbingly alive and conscious. In this
vulnerable state old certainties crumble. But he is guided by
three ghostly revenants from Harris's previous novels: Kaiser
who has become the storekeeper of the heartland; Petra a
pregnant Amerindian woman and Da Silva, the pork-knocker,
whose second death points Stevenson in the direction of a
journey that crosses the boundaries between life and death.
Harris, who was for many years a surveyor in the Guyanese
hinterland, creates a powerfully physical sense of the complex
relationship between the human and the natural worlds.

The Eye of the Scarecrow
ISBN: 9781845231644; pp. 112; pub. 2011; £8.99
With an introduction by Michael Mitchell

An unnamed diarist, writing in London, in 1963, reflects on
episodes of his life in British Guiana that profoundly altered
his vision and understanding of the world. There are childhood incidents, such as time he pushed his friend into a canal,
but finds no blame is attached to his role; there is his youthful
witnessing of a march of workers in 1948, protesting the
killing of their comrades by the police during a bitter strike,
and his momentary, but disconcerting perception that his

friend is an empty scarecrow of a man, a vision that leaves him with "a curious void of conventional everyday feeling."

There begins a radical exploration of the indeterminacy of memory and the capacity of the imagination to see beyond the everyday, to tap into the interplay between the material and the spiritual, the conscious and unconscious mind. Though Harris challenges the reader by removing the props of linear narration, he compensates by offering a poetic richness of sensuous association.

The Sleepers of Roraima & The Age of the Rainmakers
ISBN9781845231651; pp. 200; pub. 1970, 1971, 2014; £9.99
Introduction: Mark McWatt

In 1970 and 1971, Wilson Harris published two short story collections that explored the myths, fables and fragments of history of the Amerindian peoples of Guyana and the Caribbean. These are brought together in the current volume. *The Sleepers of Roraima*, subtitled "A Carib Trilogy" focuses on the ironic fate of the Caribs, the feared conquerors of other Amerindian peoples, the cannibals of European legend, but in the present the most vanished, almost extinct of all these groups. In *The Age of the Rainmakers*, each of the stories focuses on one of the groups still present in Guyana: the Macusi, Arecuna, Wapisiana and Arawaks. In the absence of reliable history, and in the face of the stereotypes attached to these people (such as stoicism or a propensity for laughter), Harris makes no attempt to write conventional fictional reconstructions of an ethnographic kind, but subjects the fragments of tribal lore to imaginative revision. His stories work towards the discovery of what is "original" in the sense of primordial in these narratives, in discovering such common patterns as the loss of innocence, the connections between sacrifice and transcendence, or even the shared identities of cannibal and Eucharistic consumption.